THE TETHERED SOUL OF EASTON GREEN

THE TETHERED SOUL OF EASTON GREEN

THE TETHERED SOUL SERIES, BOOK 1

LAURA C. REDEN

CONTENTS

THE TETHERED SOUL OF EASTON GREEN

CHAPTER 1

The first time I died was the hardest. I was a mess, not yet callused to say goodbye and overwhelmed by the fear of uncertainty. Still, it was one of my favorites . . . because that's the one in which I met Easton Green.

White knuckles gripped my steering wheel. My hands clenched tight as the tension turned to numbness. Mascara dripped from my cheeks. I lost my stomach, again. I was too young. There was so much I'd yet to see and experience. I'd never been in love.

The windshield wipers screeched louder than the stereo, and even though the heat was cranked up as high as it could go, I was still chilled to the bone. It must have been shock. Bad things happen to good people. That's what I told myself while forcing my concentration back to the road. The forest was barely visible through the condensation of my windows and the tears in my eyes. Few cars passed me on the winding two-lane road, momentarily blinding me as the wind threatened to push my truck outside of the lane. I shouldn't have been driving in my condition. Especially not with the storm. The angels must have been crying for me this dreary afternoon.

I wiped the snot from my nose on the sleeve of my forearm. I must have looked as terrible as I felt. I was a hideous wreck. Why me? What did I do to deserve this? It was the question that kept on giving. The more I thought about it, the more questions I had. Mom and Dad flashed into my mind, and my stomach dropped once more. This time, the thought came with pain—as sharp as a knife and as quick as deceit. How would I tell my parents? My brother? They would be even more devastated than I was. Certainly, it would be the worst part. I couldn't do it. I refused. Call it fear, call it denial, but I wasn't going to deal with any of it.

As I crossed the wooden arch of the New River Bridge, the silhouette of a man appeared, standing high on top the guardrails. *What was that!?* I lurched out of my trance as I slammed on the brakes. The dark phantom resided in the forefront of my mind. The truck hydroplaned, sliding recklessly until it skidded to a stop with one wheel on top of the curb.

My heart pounded. *Was I trying to kill myself!?* My hand wrapped around the rearview mirror, and I could see that he was still there, though I could barely make him out through the thick haze of the storm. I had to do something. Anything. But was this safe? I was confident the man was unwell, possibly planning to take his own life. I hesitated before unbuckling, but time was of the essence. I was going to die anyway. I would rather die a hero than whatever misery I had waiting for me in the seasons to come.

I pushed my door open and stepped out into the rain. "Stop!" I screamed, but my voice was lost in the howling wind. Rain pelted my face. "Stop!" My voice splintered. Either he didn't hear me, or he didn't care. I ran straight for him. The decision was made by my legs alone. Completely involuntary. As I parted from my truck, rain saturated my hair, and water seeped through my sneakers. The engine running, and the door gaped open. Never in a million years could I have imagined a scenario where I would run straight for a deranged stranger, but my body deceived me in more ways than one. My heartstrings pulled like those of a marionette. It was at this moment that I lost all control. Fate was simply unraveling at my feet.

"Don't do it!" I cried out to him.

Finally hearing my cries, the man turned his attention to me. He was no older than I was. His toes hung over the edge of the rail. It was a nine-hundred-foot plunge down to the river. And since this was the first rain of the year, it was sure to be particularly rocky. He would never make it. I stopped a good distance away, showing him my palms. I meant no harm. I only wanted to help.

"What?" he yelled back to me through the bellowing wind, one hand holding onto a cable for balance.

"You don't have to do this!" It sounded cliché as soon as it left my mouth, but it was true, and he needed to hear it. Unlike me, he still had choices.

He turned his focus back to the river rocks below. Taking advantage of his lack of attention, I inched my way closer. Slow and easy. "My name is Everly Beck, but everyone calls me Beck," I shouted through the rain.

I had once seen a special on tactics used to escape being held at gunpoint, and one of the tips was to let your attacker know personal details about you. Supposedly, the killer would be a little less murderous if they knew you shared common ground as dog lovers or tequila sunrise fans. Of course, this situation was different. The guy wasn't holding me at gunpoint. He wasn't trying to hurt me at all —only himself. And I hadn't seen a special on tactics to stop a suicide. I wished I had.

Still, I tried with what little information I had. "I know you're having a shitty day. I am too! We have a lot in common!" I took another gradual step forward. He looked at me, then turned to the depths below. *Shit! Too soon!*

"What makes you think I'm having a bad day?" he yelled into the distance between us.

Wasn't it obvious? "I see you're about to do something really . . ." I stopped. I didn't want to offend him in his fragile state. Who knows how much more he could take.

"What? Say it! I'm about to do something really, what?" he snapped as he let go of the cable.

"Oh, No! No! No! Don't do that!" I crouched, ready to pounce on him. But I was still too far away. After a moment of frozen fear on both sides of the exchange, I inched closer. In that moment, I was nothing more than a hunter. My focus sharp and narrow. My heart racing like a Maserati. I was more alive now than ever before, and I'd be lying if I said there wasn't a piece of me that was relieved to be worried about someone else for a change. My body began to tremble as my wet clothes clung to me, making the wind unbearable.

"Really . . . Permanent! Please, just come down from there!" The negotiation reduced to begging as I wrapped my arms tightly around my body. They offered me no warmth.

He began to laugh. I was taken aback by his outlandish sense of humor. He was anything but sane. He threw himself forward, and his feet slipped on the rail.

"No!" I screamed like never before, my voice shattered like glass on concrete. My stomach dropped as I lunged, closing the gap between us to grab him. My frozen fingers barely grasped the back of his shirt as he fell to the sidewalk. He landed on his side with a thud. My momentum continued forward, and I tripped over his body, laying me out on the ground beside him.

Our eyes met as I laid toppled over the stranger. I sucked in a quick breath as I released his shirt and retracted my hand. How did I find myself in such a compromised position with this man? The truck was far away now, but the door was still open and the stereo's faint sound drifted to us from the distance. The pounding in my chest told me I should get out of there; I should run. But I was frozen. Like the stranger before me, I was in shock. His dark hair was plastered to the side of his face, and rain collected at his chin, forming one steady stream to his chest. Like me, he was panting. Quick and shallow breaths laced with anxiety. I trembled as a strong gust of wind blew and sheets of rain pelted down on me.

Transfixed, I lingered a moment longer than I should

have. He was unusual, alright; the whole situation was. I felt something I couldn't quite put my finger on. Something I would have liked to explore longer . . . had I not felt threatened by the uncertainty of the situation.

An earsplitting clap of thunder jolted me from my trance, and I jumped to my feet. The guy continued to lay on the curb, drowning in the rain. He wasn't a threat to me or anyone but himself. He was a broken soul. He closed his eyes and let the storm wash his resignation away. I glanced back at my truck before taking pity on him.

"Can I drive you somewhere?" I asked him. The closest residence wasn't for another five miles. He couldn't walk in this weather. We were both shuddering, most likely from the cold but maybe an adrenaline overload too.

He rolled onto his back and smiled up at me. "I'd like that," he said and held out his hand. I reached down to help him to his feet. His hand was freezing, yet he still had a firm grip. He stood about a foot taller than my average height. *Was this a bad idea?* My heart was galloping, my mind racing. The whole day had been a series of unfortunate events. I hoped I would live through the night, but I wasn't sure what my fate might hold.

I started to ramble nervously. *The more he knows . . .*

"I'm a full-time student. I'm studying to become a graphic designer." I stopped abruptly, wincing when I realized that dream would never come true. "Um . . . I work at a coffee shop, mainly because they help pay for my tuition, but I really love getting free coffee too."

I unlocked my passenger's door and sat in my now drenched truck. I shut my door, but the inside was just as wet and cold as the storm outside. The heater helped to calm my nerves—ever so slightly. I pushed my dripping, ash-blond hair out of my eyes before buckling up. He hadn't said much at all, and the silence got to me.

"I didn't catch your name," I prompted him.

"Easton Green," he replied as he held his hands up to the heater.

"Nice to meet you, Easton," I said. *Nice to meet you?* Was it, though? Nice? Or was it more like I had just met him in his darkest moment?

Why did I even bother trying to be polite at this point? I frowned, racked with self-doubt. "Where am I taking you?" I asked, hating everything that came out of my mouth.

He wasn't as scary as I thought a stranger about to jump off the New River Bridge would be. He was surprisingly normal. And I was predictably awkward.

"Um, it's just up here." He vaguely pointed into the distance.

I put my truck in reverse and backed off the curb. The ride was silent, except for the windshield wipers and the random claps of thunder that made me jump in my seat. I snuck little peeks at the wet stranger to my side as I drove. What was this guy thinking? He had presumably *walked* to the bridge in the middle of a storm in a T-shirt. I hadn't seen his car or any car for that matter, and now he was getting a ride home in my beat-up red truck. How weird was this thing we called life?

I came upon the small town of Clover. Easton was looking out his rain-drizzled window; nearly all of it was covered in fog. I drove slowly, allowing him the opportunity to talk, but he didn't say anything—not even the directions to his home.

Eventually, I had to ask. "Where do you live?"

"You can just drop me off here or wherever's convenient for you." He waved his hand about.

Drop him off wherever? Was he homeless? His clothes appeared new and stylish, even in their soaked state. I couldn't drop him off at a gas station in this storm. What was I going to do? I searched the road for answers. He probably hadn't eaten for a while. Maybe he didn't have the money to buy dinner. It was a terrible situation to be in. Here I was having the worst day of my life, but I still had a roof over my head and a full belly. I still had a loving family and friends. Fleeting or not. I wasn't broken. Not yet, anyway.

I drove to a diner. "Come on, let's get some dinner. Then you can be on your way," I said, feeling somewhat responsible for the guy I found on the side of the road.

I pulled into a parking spot. It looked like we were the only ones out in this weather. Unquestionably, I was the only one with a suicidal hitchhiker for a date.

"Red Brick Diner" flickered above the entry, the *B* temporarily failing to light. Bells jingled as I opened the door, and the smell of coffee and pie wafted through the air. Red checkered accents covered the diner and screamed, *stay —but not long.* A short, curvy lady with large breasts and a name tag, on which "Sue" had been scribbled, greeted us at the door.

"Just you two?" she asked as she grabbed a couple of menus, somehow managing to never make eye contact. I get it; life can be challenging, but if you're going to work as a hostess, a fake smile would be nice.

"Yes, please," I said, but she was already walking away. We followed her to a booth in an isolated corner. "Can we start with a couple of coffees, please?" I asked Sue as we took our seats. The light blue vinyl was stained brown, and I presumed it was where kids had wiped their greasy hands instead of using a napkin.

Sue said nothing in return, but I knew she'd heard me. *Rude.*

"I don't have my wallet on me," Easton said, apologetically. He was planning on taking his life thirty minutes ago; I didn't expect him to bring cash.

"It's on me. Get whatever you want," I said and slid the menu across the table, still shaking in my wet clothes.

Sue returned with two black coffees. I was eager to feel the heat from the inside out. She slammed the mugs down on the table, and coffee spilled over the edges. Was that necessary? I frowned at the puddle around my mug.

Easton reached for his coffee, brushing up against Sue's hand. "*You* . . . have the most beautiful eyes," he said, looking up at Sue.

What? What was happening?

She melted. A high-pitched sound came from her throat. Her cheeks flushed, and a grin larger than life stretched across her face.

"Aren't you a devil!" she snickered. "Let me know when you are ready to order; I'll just be over there. Take your time. Oh, and the clam chowder soup is delicious tonight. It might warm you up some." Sue walked away with pep in her step.

Who *was* this guy? I hid my smirk behind my coffee cup. Secondhand embarrassment was real. I knew my cheeks were as red as Sue's. And with my pale, washed-out complexion, the red in my cheeks was a noticeable pop of color. Even so, my emotions would not go unnoticed.

Easton looked at his menu as if nothing out of the ordinary had happened. Just another day for this young man. I stared at him in wonder. Something was weird about him. And I was nothing less than intrigued.

I wanted to know what was going on in his head. Staring at him certainly wasn't going to give me the answers I desired. If anything, it was going to make *me* look like the crazy one. The thunder clapped, and I jumped in my seat, spilling a few drops of coffee on my already soaked jeans.

"This storm is wild, huh?" It was the best I had. Making small talk with a stranger was hard work.

"The storm?" Easton looked out the diner window for a brief moment before continuing. "It's quite the rager . . . Why do you think people like to talk about the weather?" Easton asked before placing his menu to the side of the table.

What? Why was he challenging me? Why couldn't he just say something generic about the rain? It's crazy or I can't believe it . . . anything.

"I don't know. Because it's interesting?" I couldn't help myself from sounding sarcastic. But I *did* think the weather was interesting. Why else would people stare out their windows and watch the lightning dance across the sky?

"They talk about the weather because it's usually the only obvious parallel topic between them. It's happening all around them; therefore, they know they have something in common to talk to one another about," he said, staring at me, his eyes full of intent. And for the first time, I realized how remarkable they were. Light blue like the glaciers in the Antarctic, but surprisingly warm.

I suppose what he said was true. I had never thought of it like that.

"But you and I have something else in common, don't we?" he asked.

CHAPTER 2

Something in common? Did we? Was he dying too? Being so entranced in thought, I was startled when Sue asked for our order.

"I'll try the soup as you recommended. Thank you." Easton smiled at Sue as he handed her the menu off the table. Sue's cheeks turned red all over again. She had a crush. Easton was probably the first guy to show her attention in a long time. Had he not been so much younger than her, I'm sure she would've made a move. Probably with me sitting right across from him.

"Same. Thank you," I said, forcing a smile.

Sue didn't like me, and she showed it when she snatched the menu out of my hand and turned sharp on her heels. I was used to it by now. Most women didn't like me. I'd heard several times from friends that I was different than what they had expected of me. It must be my face. The way I carry myself. An invisible pheromone I put out. Something . . .

Easton's glacial eyes were burning a hole through me. Waiting for my answer.

"We do? What is it?" I asked, both intrigued and worried in equal parts. Did I want to know what I had in common with a suicidal homeless man?

"You're having a shitty day. You said so yourself, back at the bridge," Easton said, relaxed here at the diner as if he wasn't wearing wet clothes or sitting with me, a stranger. Why was he so comfortable? This conversation alone was freaking me out. I shuddered as water from my hair dripped onto my chest.

"You're right. I did say that." I didn't want to talk about it. I wasn't ready. "You clearly are having a shittier day than I am. Do *you* want to talk about it?" I asked him. I had to take the focus off of me. I wasn't the one ready to end everything, after all. I still had some fight left in me. As brief as it may be.

"I'm not having a bad day. Thank you, Sue." I jumped again. Easton helped guide his soup down to the table. *Where did she come from!?*

Sue placed my soup down in front of me. Her thumb dug deep into my clam chowder. I sighed, not able to thank her. Chills ran down my spine after hearing her thumb pop out of her mouth like a kiss. She was probably attempting to flirt with Easton. It was nothing but gross. And now my soup was tainted.

"But if you want to talk about what *you're* going through, I'd listen," Easton said before digging into his soup.

Me? Like I was the crazy one here? Huh . . . I guess it was a possibility.

"I don't want to talk about it." But as soon as I said it, the silence was deafening. My leg bounced uncontrollably under the table. All the tension I had been carrying around with me grew heavy. I didn't want to talk about it. But I needed to.

"You're not the only one dying, you know. We all are. Just at different speeds," Easton said casually.

I gasped. How did he know that? Was he a mind reader? A clairvoyant? I felt incredibly vulnerable, like he could see right through me. I tightened my wet jacket around me.

"How," I started.

"You told me back at the bridge. Remember? You were disgusted with me and how I could be throwing away my life when you didn't have the choice to keep yours." Easton paused, taking me in.

I didn't remember saying any of it to him. But it was exactly how I felt. My thumb-dipped soup stared back at me. I pushed the bowl away; I wasn't hungry anyhow. My memory must have lapsed at the peak of the adrenaline rush. I furrowed my eyebrows at the distaste of feeling exposed. He was the first person to know. I didn't feel as bad as I thought I might, though. Perhaps it was because he was a stranger. A stranger who had his own baggage and misfortunes. Like me, he couldn't possibly judge; he had no grounds for it. I felt his gaze on me, and I shrugged, unable to look back at him.

"What is it? Cancer?" he asked as if he were checking

the flavor of a chocolate candy before popping it in his mouth. He returned his gaze to the meal before him.

I reached up to my neck and traced the lump with my fingertips. A small sound escaped my throat as if an admission of guilt.

Easton nodded before settling his crystal eyes on me. For a brief moment, I felt understood. I must be at a really low point in my life to feel like the only one who understands me is a soaking wet stranger sitting across from me in a stained vinyl booth.

"I've had it for some time." I looked everywhere but directly at him. The words fell out of my mouth. "I ignored all of the symptoms. I thought I was too young for something like this. It's my fault, really. I had a biopsy years ago, but it was inconclusive. They wanted me to come back for a repeat, but I thought there was no way in hell I was having a needle jabbed into my throat again." I winced at the memory of the pressure on my throat and the pain in my ears.

"I thought they just wanted my money, so I ignored it." My eyes drifted off to a faraway land. I felt empty inside. "And now, it's too late. There's nothing they can do." I found it odd that my eyes had begun to water since I felt nothing inside. In one moment, the truth was too much to bear, and then in the next, it was so far removed from reality that it couldn't possibly be my life. My fingertips traced my coffee mug handle.

Easton was the best kind of listener. The one who actually paid attention. No judgment. He understood, and he didn't try to fix anything or interrogate me with questions. He just gave me a warm body to talk to so I wasn't alone and the time to reflect on what lay deep inside. Had I been telling this to my parents, they would have jumped down my throat, grilled me on specific details, and made me feel guilty for not taking better care of myself. Guilty for taking their little girl away from them. Or perhaps, I would make myself think that all on my own.

Easton was gazing down into his coffee mug. He appeared sad. I knew that I was a downer, but somehow, I felt a little lighter after telling someone my secret.

"I'm sorry," I said. "I just—"

"Don't be sorry. It's life. You can't apologize for that," Easton said, his forehead creasing in defeat.

He was wise beyond his years—an old soul. I wondered what happened in his life to make him break. His hair was drying to an unruly dark mess that swept into his eyebrows. The reddish-brown bags under his blue eyes made me think that he hadn't slept in weeks. His skin was pale like mine. But unlike mine, which was genetic; his skin appeared white due to a lack of sunlight. I wondered if he was too far gone for the mood-enhancing benefits of vitamin D.

Sue came to our table with a check and a slice of blackberry pie "on the house." I dug out my wallet while she talked to Easton about the storm. I tried to hide my amusement. He didn't challenge her in the way he did me. Maybe he didn't care to. Sue took the card from my hand as she thanked Easton. I might as well have been invisible to her. It was so ridiculous; had it been a different day, I might have laughed out loud.

I caught myself wondering what Easton would look like with a smile. Though he wasn't my type: tall, slender . . . emotional. Challenging and intelligent. I was always attracted to the meatheads. The ones with more testosterone than they knew what to do with. The ones that had basic needs and basic brains. And subsequently, remarkable bodies. I never needed more than eye candy. I had fun with my friends, and I could always talk to my mom if needed. Still, I questioned what a smile would do for him.

"Are you going to be OK?" Easton asked me.

I found it odd that I was thinking the same about him. Somehow, he made me forget about my situation. If only for a few short moments.

"Yeah. I mean, until I'm not." How was I supposed to answer a question like that? I assumed it would be something I would learn over the next couple of weeks through trial and error.

"Are you?" I asked.

Sue crept into my peripheral vision. She wasn't going to spook me this time.

"Here you go. Just sign there." Sue handed me a pen with the receipt. I was tempted not to leave her a tip, but I played nice. "Don't be a stranger now, you hear?" Sue giggled, eyes set on Easton as her cheeks turned red once more. She retreated to the kitchen.

"I think she likes you."

Easton shot me a smile that did something to my insides. A weird flutter stirred inside.

I guess this was it. I'd lingered long enough. It was time

I said goodbye. I grabbed my bag and slid out of the booth. Easton stayed put.

"Are you sure you're going to be OK?" I asked, feeling guilty about leaving him.

"I'll be just fine. It was nice to meet you, Everly," Easton said with a warm expression. How come it didn't sound out of place when he said it? I glanced around the diner. It's not like I had another choice. I wasn't going to bring him home like a stray dog. It was weird I even considered it. He pulled the pie in a little closer and picked up the fork.

"OK. You too," I managed to say. It felt off, but I didn't know why.

I turned around and walked out of the diner. The draft sent a shudder through my body as I opened the door. The rain pelted down on me, soaking me once more. I tried to shield my head as I ran to my truck. I cranked the heater up before stealing one last glance at the peculiar stranger I had met on the bridge. The waitress was making her way back to him. Huh . . . probably going to talk to him about the weather some more. I pulled away and continued homeward. But this time, I thought about Easton instead of my diagnosis.

I pulled into my driveway. It was my parents' house. They'd bought it as a rental. When I was old enough to move out, the place was vacant. It was only fitting that I moved in. The dead potted plants were finally getting some water with the rain. Mom would be happy about that. I knew they would get a drink at some point in time. Maybe they would grow back, and she would never know I neglected them in the first place. I ran to the door and fumbled with my keys. My hands were wet and slippery. Yeti impatiently barked inside.

When I finally opened the door, she jumped and barked rambunctiously, her bear-like body intermittently bumping into me. I peeled off my jacket and kicked off my wet shoes. They joined a shoe graveyard where five or six pairs lay scattered by the front door. I placed my bag on a small entry table before greeting Yeti. But her excitement only made me sad. What would she do after I was gone? Maybe my brother would take her. I would have to start bringing her over to his house to break her in slowly. Get her used to the idea. I padded barefoot to the heater. Even the carpet was cold under my feet. I tried not to think about it, but everywhere I looked was one more thing I had to deal with now, or my parents would have to later. I would have to start scaling back my already empty house.

Late that night, I found myself nose-deep in a hot bath. As the chill in my bones lifted, the heat helped to calm my aching heart, though tears continued to flow down my face. I didn't know how I would make it through the next few months of my life. The *last* few months of my life. I didn't know much about the emotional stages I would be going through, but I knew acceptance was one of them, and I couldn't wait to get there. If I could just get there.

My doctor's voice, low and callused, played through my head. "Terminal." Like a punch to the gut. By the time he said, "metastasized," I was barely listening to anything but the ringing in my ears. I winced. The punch was fake, but the pain was real.

With my eyes closed tight, I saw something different

altogether, and I welcomed the change in thought. I saw Easton's rain-soaked shoes hanging over the rail of the New River Bridge. This, too, pained me. But in a different way. Without knowing Easton, I recognized that he was special. And the world needed special people; they were the glue that held the rest of us together.

It wasn't fair that he would have considered jumping. Regret boiled up inside of me. My eyes opened and focused on my red toenail polish—chipped fire hydrant red, nearly two weeks old. I should have stayed at the diner. I should have done more to help him. I played my regrets over and over in my head until the bathwater turned cold, and I became chilled once more.

CHAPTER 3

When my alarm sounded the next morning, I picked up my phone and threw it against my wall as hard as I could. As luck would have it, the alarm didn't stop. I tossed my heavy blue corduroy comforter off me and lay motionless while Yeti bumped her nose into me and bashed her tail into my nightstand. Why do I need to go to work anyway? Why do I need to do anything? I could just lie here and wither away.

As tempting as it was, the beeping of my alarm was maddening, and the dog needed to go out. I suppose I could be a contributing member of society for one day longer.

I pet Yeti on the head as I retrieved my phone from a pile of dirty laundry I'd been planning on doing for days. The screen had broken on impact. I sighed. Usually, I would tell myself, 'It only gets better from here,' but today was different, and I knew that was no longer true.

I took out a pair of crisp jeans from my closet; they were

the only ones left that were clean. I pulled them on, jumping several times to get them over my butt. They would loosen up as the day went on, but straight out of the wash, they were much too tight. It was typical for cheap jeans to make a girl feel out of shape and start her day off with more self-esteem issues than any one person should have in a twenty-four-hour period.

I slipped my embroidered Fresh Grounds T-shirt over my head and brushed my teeth. The only thing I enjoyed about working was unlimited caffeine. And today, I needed it more than ever. I owned a coffee pot, but I usually got my coffee from work, even on my days off. The little shop was on my way to school, making it convenient for me to drop in on my way out of town. I sighed, looking into the mirror before deciding to embrace my pale, bare face, but I drew the line with naked eyes; I coated my lashes in black mascara. I knew my cheeks would pinken throughout the day, so I skipped blush and finished with a lip gloss that would darken my naturally rosy lips, ever so slightly. Without it, my face would look like a ghost. *How ironic.* After parting my hair to the side, I pulled back my light blond strands into a messy bun at the nape of my neck. It would be covered by my Fresh Grounds trucker hat anyway.

I said goodbye to Yeti and threw my apron over my shoulder before heading out the door. I surprised myself with how typical my morning was. When would it all change? It was difficult to imagine that one day I would be too feeble to serve coffee.

The storm had subsided, but the dampness and chill

remained. A cool breeze blew, causing me to pinch my jacket closed around my neck. I started my truck and waited impatiently for it to warm up. The steering wheel was like ice under my hands, and my breath was visible. I switched the station on my stereo about every fifteen seconds. Every song made me feel *something*, and every emotion reminded me of my limited time. It was in my best interest not to tap into my feelings before work. If I did, I might never find my way out. I was about to pull into the parking lot before I turned off the stereo all together. I figured that music and I would have to part ways.

The warm air welcomed me from the post-thunderstorm breeze outside. But nothing was better than the smell of fresh-ground coffee. I inhaled deeply, trying to get even a morsel of caffeine in my system. Used books lined the shelves behind two old leather recliners. Fresh Grounds coffee mugs and T-shirts sat on the shelves for sale. Even though the place was packed, I recognized Greg's camel-colored jacket. He was about fourth in line. There was always a line here at Fresh Grounds, and Greg always seemed to be standing in it. He was one of our regular customers. We had tons of regulars, but he was one of the few I enjoyed serving.

I swung the bar door open and whispered my order to Lindsay as I passed by. She was in the middle of crafting marvelous latte art. Nobody could turn milk into art the way Lindsay could—not even the owner. Lindsay and I were longtime friends. We applied for the job together when the coffee shop opened up. Luckily, we both got a job and often worked together. My days were better when she was on schedule with me. I stashed my bag in the backroom and slipped my apron over my head.

"Hi, I can help you over here." I tied my apron behind my back as I stepped up to the open cash register.

A mom and two beautiful twin teenagers stepped up to my register. They must have been passing through Clover. A road trip, perhaps? I'd never seen them before.

"Good morning, I'll take two coffees with room for cream. To go please," the mother said.

As I entered the info into my register, one of the twins took a step forward. Her long blond hair was stunning. A pang of jealousy rippled through my body, and I hated myself for it. She had it all, though: beauty, family, and from the looks of it, money. She was young—maybe sixteen. I bet she was the "it" girl at her high school.

"I'll have a grande caramel frappe, make that half caff, and extra whipped cream. Make sure you drizzle the caramel on the inside of the cup before pouring in the frappe. Oh! And a cheese danish—hot," the girl said as she raised an eyebrow. Huh, it figures she was entitled, too. One medium caramel frap . . . got it.

The second twin, a spitting image of her sister, stepped forward. "Um, I'll have the same." She looked away quickly, not making eye contact. It was clear that she wasn't the dominant twin. I looked between her and her sister before feeling bad for the girl. She lacked the confidence a girl needed to survive high school. It was as if her sister had absorbed it all in the womb and left her with nothing.

"Oh, and can you make it full caffeine? Sorry!" She shouldn't need to apologize for changing her order. I wish I could tell her to stand tall, take up space, and order her caffeine with confidence!

"Not a problem, and what's the name?"

"Hadley—" she said.

"Holly!" The sister barked from behind her.

I paused and looked at both of them before writing Hadley on all four cups. Lindsay slipped my coffee next to me, and I gave her a quick pat on the shoulder. The bitter americano soothed my parched throat. I would have a sugar-riddled frappe on break, but breakfast was always black and bitter. Much like prying myself out of bed in the morning.

"Good morning, Greg. How are you doing today?" I asked as he approached.

He had his camel jacket on as he did every single day of the year. I wasn't sure that I would recognize him without it. The doorbells jingled, and the line grew longer. My day had just started, and I already needed a break.

"I'm good, Beck. How are you today?" he asked as he opened his wallet.

It stung. How was I? I was terrible. Frightened. I was barely holding it together. And as of an hour ago, I was doing so with a shattered cell phone.

"Oh, same old, same old," I said. My life wasn't anything special before yesterday. What I would give to have my mediocre life back now.

"I'll have the regular. Oh, and Carol wants a slice of banana bread this morning," he said while flipping through the cash in his hands.

He was in his seventies, and he'd been coming here

nearly every day since we opened. He was a good man with a kind heart.

"Here, keep the change." He placed a ten-dollar bill on the counter.

"Thank you, Greg. Have a nice day today. And tell Carol we said hello," I replied.

I survived the morning rush and was beyond thankful for my break. We weren't supposed to take breaks at the same time as other employees, but we only had a couple of customers, so Lindsay took the seat next to me. Her natural blond hair was dyed black. It made her blue eyes look electric. Her face was round and youthful, and her whinnied laugh was contagious. But today, I was immune to her infectious spunk. I had hardly been listening when she updated me on the potty training she had been doing with Capone, her new puppy.

"Hey, what's wrong?" Lindsay reached out and pushed on my knee.

Shit! My throat began to burn, and my eyes prepared for waterworks. *Hold it together!*

"Nothing!" I rubbed my eyes. "Allergies. They're driving me nuts," I said.

Lindsay bought it. I was pretty sure that I could pass off many of my symptoms on allergies. That's what I had told myself for the better part of the year, and I believed it, myself.

"That sucks. But hey, it could be worse." Lindsay shrugged while scooping whipped cream out of her drink with her straw. "I mean, people are out there dying with cancer and shit."

The blood drained from my face. I almost felt like I could throw up. I jolted to my feet.

"I gotta use the restroom before my break is over!" I blurted out and stammered to the bathroom.

"But your break just started!" Lindsay called out behind me.

I had been looking forward to my break all morning, but now that I had it, I wished I was working my shift. I couldn't talk to Lindsay about her squishy faced puppy. I lacked the appropriate excitement. And I sure as hell couldn't talk to her about . . . I don't know, allergies? Because that went south really quick!

I washed my hands under the warm water for far too long, trapped in the restroom because beyond those doors was a reality that I didn't have the tools to face. Again, I hadn't seen that tv special. I couldn't face my friend; she would know something was terribly wrong. But I couldn't hide in the bathroom all day either.

I dried my hands and left the comfort I'd found in the privacy of the restroom. A few more customers had wandered in, and Lindsay was working the cash register. I was thankful she hadn't been waiting for me to return to our conversation.

I was headed to clean up the mess I left on break when Easton's voice penetrated my mind.

"Easton," he said.

"Thank you. That will be right out," Lindsay said while writing on a cup.

Easton turned to walk away. I saw the side of his face and automatically looked away. What was he doing here?

Would he blow my cover? What was I going to say to him?

"Everly?" Easton called out. I froze midway to the frappe I had barely touched on my break. Easton snuck up behind me. I grabbed my drink and stood to my full height before turning around.

"Hey! You found me!" I said, immediately regretting it when I saw his reaction.

His blue eyes filled with . . . what was that? Pity? I didn't need sympathy. Especially not from him. I took him in from head to toe. His hair remained unruly, even in its dried state, and he was wearing a wool grey trench coat and blue jeans. This time, he didn't look homeless—not in the least. Did I make that part up? Judging by the sunglasses hanging from the neck of his shirt, I would even go as far as to say he was well-off.

"That I did! How are you doing today?" Easton asked. His eyes scanning me up and down, a hint of interest in the corner of his eyes.

I felt overexposed. He knew my deepest, darkest secret. And now he was standing in front of me at my coffee shop, in front of Lindsay. It made my secret real. Tangible almost. I couldn't hide from it in the bathroom as long as he was there with me. I nervously glanced around, hoping nobody could hear us.

"I'm good!" I squeaked. I sighed and rolled my eyes. Sometimes I was the most exhausting person. We both knew I was lying.

Easton shook his head, understanding I wasn't ready to make my cancer a reality. He sat down on the old leather recliner in front of me and crossed his ankle over his knee. There was something about him that made me want to open up. I looked back to Lindsay again. She had the line of customers under control. I sat down on the edge of the other recliner and leaned into Easton.

"It's just that nobody knows. I can't tell them. But, I can't live a lie either." It came tumbling out of me. "I'm barely holding it together! And I don't know how long I can pretend I have allergies!" My eyes begged the stranger I met on the bridge for answers. I don't know why I thought he would have them. But I did.

Easton uncrossed his leg and leaned forward to meet me. He rested his elbows on his knees and clasped his hands together.

"You should tell your friends and family. You should tell everyone. I think it would help you cope with it in the long run. But start with your family," he said.

I thought about telling my mom, but she would fall apart immediately. How could that be good for anyone? Deep down, I knew he was right, though. I shouldn't keep it a secret.

"I'm sorry. I didn't even ask you how you were. How are you today?" I took a sip of my frappe, and my nerves started to calm as our conversation pivoted.

Lindsay walked over and placed Easton's latte on the table. It wasn't our typical practice to bring customers their coffee. Instead, we would call out their names and place their order on the bar for pickup. I hoped Easton didn't see her wink at me before she walked away. It's not what she thought; this was the furthest thing possible from a date. I would have some explaining to do.

"Today's a great day, now that I found you." Easton smiled as he buried his face in his mug. Was he flirting with me?

I laughed out loud. It was the first genuine laugh I had since my diagnosis, and as soon as I realized it, my smile faded. It was bittersweet.

"Don't do that," Easton said.

"Don't do what?" I asked him, shocked that he would tell me what to do, and a little fearful that he was in my head.

He leaned in again. "Don't cheat yourself out of happiness. You still have plenty of time to laugh. And you deserve it too." His forehead creased with his serious tone. It was true. *Everything* this guy said was true! I found myself nodding over and over again like a bobblehead as his words sank in. It was something I would need to remember.

I snapped myself out of his piercing gaze and looked down at my watch. My break had ended some time ago.

"I've got to go back to work," I said as I stood up and collected my trash. "Will I see you again?" I asked, keeping my eyes on the table. I didn't know what to make of him. He was confusing to me on many levels. But the one thing I did know was that he was the only person that understood me at the moment. And that brought me an immeasurable amount of comfort.

"I think I could make that happen." Easton smiled up at

me, and I felt my cheeks flush. The door jingled as my mom walked through the door.

"Mom!" I blurted.

"Mom?" Easton said with curiosity as he looked over his shoulder.

CHAPTER 4

My mom wore a large cozy wrap that was more of a blanket than a cardigan. She had pale blond hair highlighted with silver strands. Her light green eyes were identical to mine.

I stepped away from Easton and gave my mom an awkward hug. "Hey, what are you doing here?" I asked.

"What? Am I not allowed to visit my daughter at her work? Come on! You haven't been returning my calls; what do you expect?" She held out her hands to signify the lack of options. Another customer came in behind her. Like building blocks, my apprehension was stacking higher, and higher.

"Sorry, Mom, I've had . . . a headache." I quickly glanced at Easton, who was raising his eyebrows in judgment but pretending not to eavesdrop.

"A headache! You can't call your mother because you have a headache? Geez, Beck, I was worried about you!" Mom said as she reached in for another hug.

"Sorry! I'll try harder to return your calls," I mumbled before glancing back at Lindsay. "Hey, I need to get to work. Can we talk later?" I asked, glancing around the room so that my eyes could land on Easton for a split moment.

Just do it. Be brave. "I, um, have something I want to talk to you about." My voice quivered.

"You do? Why don't you come over tonight for dinner? 5:00," Mom said—more of a statement than a question.

I grimaced. It was too soon.

"Tonight?" I tried to buy myself some time to think of an excuse.

"Yes, tonight! Your brother is coming tonight, and he is bringing his girlfriend. You can tell us your big news then. 5:00!" she said before lowering her voice. "Now, can you get me a cappuccino with a foamy heart on top?"

I sighed. I couldn't tell my family the news while my brother's girlfriend was present. I nodded, deflated and discouraged.

"Yeah. Just one sec, Mom," I said.

Mom always whispered when she asked for free coffee, even though I told her it was OK with the owner. I would have to ask Lindsay to do the heart for me, though, as I always screwed them up. I turned on my heels and headed back to work. I was utterly embarrassed that Easton had heard the whole exchange. Worse yet, my stomach dropped when I peered out from the espresso machine and caught Easton chatting with my mom. She looked amused, which wasn't saying much. Everything excited my mom. The world could be raining acid, and she would stare at it and marvel over mother nature.

He wouldn't tell her my secret, would he? The milk screamed as I started the frother. I watched my mom chuckle as I tapped the metal frothing cup with my palm to check for the perfect temperature. I guess she wouldn't be laughing if he told her. That was the only indication I had that my secret was safe.

"Hey, Lindsay, can you make a heart on top of this cappuccino?" I asked. She made me watch her for the hundredth time. But no matter how many times I watched *or practiced* with soapy dyed water, my latte art never got better. Lindsay executed a perfect heart, then took it a step further and made a swan, too.

"Show-off."

I slipped a coffee sleeve over the cup and grabbed a lid, eager to interrupt Easton and my mother from their chat.

"Mom!" I called from much too far away. "Mom, I've got your cappuccino, and Lindsay even made you a swan," I said, reaching the coffee out before I even approached her.

It worked. She took a couple of steps away from Easton and met me halfway.

"See? Isn't it pretty?" I said before slipping the lid on for her.

"Oh, I just *love* that . . . see what I did there? *Love*, and it has a heart . . ." Mom elbowed me in the ribs. It was so stupid it almost made me laugh, which reminded me of Easton's comment about cheating myself from happiness. I had a long road ahead of me . . . or, actually, maybe not.

"OK, Mom. 5:00 it is. I'll see you tonight," I said as I

hugged my mom goodbye and tried to usher her out of my coffee shop before any further embarrassment could happen.

Mom resisted as she turned to Easton. "Goodbye, dear. Nice talking to you!" She waved her hand frantically at him. What on earth did he say to her? I frowned. I didn't have time for riddles, and that man puzzled me like no other.

"I'll be heading out too," Easton said, standing and joining my mother. "I'll walk you out." He turned to me and smiled. I didn't know what was behind his dimples, but I would have given just about anything to figure it out. I gave him an icy glare, but it only encouraged him more.

"Oh! That would be lovely!" Mom turned to me and winked as if she could still rope in the men. I shook my head and watched the two of them walk away.

"You have a lovely daughter," Easton said to my mom just loud enough for me to hear him. What was happening? I was about ninety percent sure he wouldn't tell her. I bit my lip, staring at the door as it closed behind them. Whatever this was, it was outside of my control.

"Beck! A little help here?" Lindsay called out. I grimaced when I saw the line had grown, and the customers were becoming upset. I must have been so wrapped up in thought that I didn't notice them come in. I hurried back to work. The hectic flow of customers didn't allow time for Lindsay to grill me on my odd behavior or the guy that I spent the rest of my break with. I found myself coming up with answers to her hypothetical questions while I worked. *He's just a guy I met the other day . . . No, I don't like him . . . I don't know why he was talking to my mother.* But she never asked. Not today, at least.

It was a long day at work, but this was just the beginning. The real work was ahead of me yet. I sat in the comfort of my truck in my parent's driveway, not yet ready to go inside. I was tired and emotional. Maybe I should just say I don't feel well and go home? The stomach flu *was* going around. My eyebrows raised as I considered the possibility of the lie.

Carter knocked on my window, and I jumped a mile high. If I had not used the restroom before leaving work, I might have peed my pants—just a little.

Instead of getting out of the truck, I stayed put and rolled my window down.

"Hey, dork," my brother said. He was holding his girlfriend's hand. I looked her over. Her dress was too frilly. Too short. I didn't like her.

"Oh my God. You must be Beck!" the girl said in a high-pitched tone.

"Actually, it's Everly." I corrected her. My brother frowned at my response.

"What are you even doing out here?" he asked. It was a valid question. One I didn't have an answer to.

I looked around my truck. "I'm just . . . I just got off work! So, I'm fixing my makeup."

He frowned, but his girlfriend understood. "Go on. I'll be inside in a minute."

He turned to walk away, and his girlfriend's high heels clacked on the driveway after him. It was too late to fake the stomach flu now. I pulled the bun out of my hair and shook the strands loose. A fresh aroma of coffee escaped my locks. At least I didn't work in a pho restaurant. Everyone loved the smell of coffee, right?

I walked to the front door, admiring the Japanese Boxwood bushes my parents had recently planted. The moment I placed my hand on the doorknob, my heart sank. I was weak, and I wanted to run away. I'd hide under the covers of my bed and waste away to nothing. One step in front of the other, I entered my childhood home, carrying my burden, heavy on my shoulders. The house was dark; no windows in the entryway. I passed the piano I'd taken lessons on as a child and failed to play since. Now it did nothing but collect dust—another manifestation of my failure. It took everything I had to enter the lively kitchen. Mom was blabbing about how pretty Carter's girlfriend was, and I could hear my dad talking to my brother about some hockey game. I wasn't sure where I fit in, but at least I showed up. Sometimes, that was the hardest part.

"Hey, Mom. I'm here." I held my arms out for a hug.

As if it wasn't hard enough to step foot into the kitchen, she burst into laughter.

"Oh, honey! Long day? You forgot to take your apron off!" Mom pointed at me as she chuckled. I looked down, disappointed, and ripped the thing off of my head.

"Hey, babe. Look, she forgot to take her apron off! I think she needs a drink!" Mom continued.

"OK, Mom. We get it. Yes, it's been a long day. Hey,

Pop!" I called out to my dad as I threw my apron on the countertop.

The girlfriend stood awkwardly off to the side as I hugged my mom. I felt bad for her, even though I thought my brother could do better.

"Hi. I'm sorry I didn't catch your name," I said as I held my hand out to greet her.

She held her hands out wide, "I'm a hugger!" she said as she wrapped her arms around me for a fake hug. "I'm Chloe!" she said as she rubbed my back with her fingers only.

"I like your dress, Chloe." This time, it was a white lie, and those were OK by me. In all honesty, I did like her frilly white dress. The pink flowers were a cute pop of girly color. But it wasn't summer, and it looked like it had shrunk in the wash. Chloe smiled wide, showing red lipstick smudged on her freakishly white teeth. *Should I tell her?* I glanced at Carter, and our eyes met; he'd taken the time to put gel in his dirty blond hair. It always looked darker when he did that. His smile was genuine. I brought my attention back to Chloe before me. *Nah, I won't tell her.*

"So, Beck," she started.

"Everly." I corrected her. This girl would probably never earn the right to call me Beck.

"Sorry, Everly. I know it's weird, but even your brother calls you Beck. Well, when he's not calling you dork-face, or whatever. So, I'm just used to it. Maybe people will even call me Beck one day!" Chloe laughed, but I found her comment more disturbing than funny. Beck was a family name. Several of our friends had grown up calling us Beck.

Sometimes it was confusing, but it was always an honor. I excused myself for that drink my mom had mentioned.

I walked over to the small counter space where we used to store the computer when I was a child. Now, it was filled with booze. I didn't want anything too strong. I knew I would need to drive myself home tonight. The sooner I could get out of here, the better. But I still needed something to take the edge off. I glanced over my shoulder at my mom. She held up a spatula covered in spaghetti sauce while she spoke to Chloe, a glass of red wine by her side. Red wine it was. I poured myself a half glass. I would have to see how the next fifteen minutes played out before helping myself to the other half.

My dad came up behind me and placed his strong hands on my shoulders, giving them a tight squeeze. The man didn't know his own strength.

"Easy, Pops, you're going to break me!" I spun around and swatted at his chest before hugging him.

"You're looking thin. You don't have weight to lose, my dear. You better eat up tonight," he said, just as he always did.

"I will. Don't worry." I said as I looked away. I knew he would pick up on my uncertainty if our eyes met. I swallowed the lump in my throat and turned the attention to the new girl.

"So, Pops, what do you make of her?" I gestured towards Chloe with my wine glass. She was laughing with my mom. A fake laugh, no doubt, but Mom didn't notice. Either that or she didn't care. She just loved attention any which way it came from.

Dad turned to watch the show. "She seems nice, you know? We've just gotta get to know her." He gave her the benefit of the doubt. He always saw the glass as half full. My mom did too. I'm not sure how I fell so far from the tree.

"Don't you think her dress is a little much?" I raised my eyebrows and took a swig of my wine. Not typically one for stirring the pot, I sure did have something against the girl. Maybe it was that her dress was too short. Her lipstick too loud. Her breasts too perky. Or perhaps, it was the fact that I was dying, and she was not. I shrugged my shoulders to brush off the thought. *It was definitely her chest.*

Dad laughed. "Oh, honey. You're never going to think a girl is good enough for your brother!" he squeezed my shoulder once more.

"Ah!" I shimmied out of his grip. That wasn't true, though. There was one girl that I thought was good enough for him. I took my last sip of wine. *That was quick.* We hadn't even started dinner. I poured myself the other half. I would take it easy.

After some more small talk and fake laughter, we all took a seat at the dinner table. I was blessed with the guest seat, the one I liked to call "the short chair." I sat about six full inches lower than the rest of my family, and I had to straddle the table legs. At this point, the stomach flu was looking pretty good. I would rather be wallowing in the bathtub alone than sitting in the short chair, watching Chloe win over my family with her lipstick teeth.

Carter tapped his fork along the side of his water glass.

"I have an announcement to make. Chloe and I are getting married!"

"What!" I blurted out.

Chloe stopped clapping her hands when she took in my expression. Everyone stopped and stared at me.

"I mean . . . when?" I felt the heat cross my face and run down my back. I took another swig of wine which emptied my glass. I equally needed more and needed to drive my sorry self home. Now would be preferable.

"Well, we were thinking of April or May. Chloe wants to do it at the Bonnie Ranch inside the red barn," Carter said, and Chloe squealed, followed by more clapping.

April was a matter of weeks away. It was too soon. He didn't even know the girl. Why was I the only one to see this? I stabbed my fork into a meatball while my mind tried to comprehend this unfortunate turn of events. I caught my dad's empathic eye from across the table. He knew I didn't like the idea. And from the look on his face, he didn't either. But my mom was another story. She was thrilled to have wedding bells in her future. She wanted grandchildren.

They were going on about what flowers Chloe liked and who she might be able to snag for a photographer around here when I couldn't take it any longer.

I abruptly stood up. The short chair fell behind me. Making a scene was the last thing I wanted to do. Everyone was staring at me, again. This whole day had been one cluster of ill-fated events. In that moment, I thought for one second. I should just say it. I should say I have cancer. My hands balled up into fists.

"Oh, honey! I'm so sorry! You had news to share with

everyone too!" Mom was trying to help, but that made it so much worse.

A cold sweat broke out across my neck and chest. *Say it! Just say it!* Carter rocked back in his full-sized chair and locked his hands behind his head.

"I . . . I have . . ." Mom had picked up Chloe's repulsive mannerisms in the blink of an eye. She silently clapped, encouraging me to say it. She looked so happy. Carter and Chloe, while making the biggest mistake of their lives, were happy too. I couldn't bring myself to do it. These people were *cheerful* people, made of light and positivity. I couldn't sweep them up in my tornado of illness. So, I did what I had been doing a lot lately: I lied—a *white* lie.

"I have . . . a boyfriend!" I faked a big smile and clapped silently.

I'd never *hated* myself more.

CHAPTER 5

"A boyfriend! I knew it! I'm going to be a grandma!" Mom waved her hands in the air like she had just won the lottery. Not one potential for grandbabies but two.

"A grandma? No, Mom, just a boyfriend!" I cleared the air, and relief washed over Dad's face.

"Oh, I know that, but first comes love, then comes marriage . . . then comes the baby in the baby carriage!" Mom was having the best night.

I rolled my eyes. Carter and I shared an exasperated look. Mom could be a bit much at times. The alcohol didn't help.

"She's not pregnant, dear! She's just got a boyfriend!" Dad looked up at me. "He's just a boyfriend, *right*?"

"Right! God, you guys. *Just* a boyfriend!"

Good Lord, these people! If this was how they reacted to my first real (and by *real*, I mean *fake*) boyfriend, then I didn't want to see what would happen when I told them I was dying!

"Oh, babe, you have to see him! He is *so* cute! And he's a charmer that one!" Mom said.

"Wait. What?" I asked, still standing.

"Easton, he's the most wonderful young man! I met him today at Fresh Grounds," Mom said.

My stomach dropped. Easton? My boyfriend? I scowled. I tried to see what my mom had seen at the coffee shop. Easton and I talking during my break. It must have looked like we were dating. What did he say to her when he walked her out? My eyes searched the table. It was all too much to take in. Or was it?

Maybe it could work? Maybe, I wouldn't have to tell them at all? They could be ignorantly blissful. Everyone could focus on the wedding instead of my health. Hell, I could even pretend that I didn't know I was sick in the first place! We would never have to talk about our feelings, and we could avoid the sad sympathy looks all together. My mind raced as I mindlessly rubbed my neck. It was a plan born out of fear, yet I saw no other way.

"Are you just going to stand there dreaming about your dork boyfriend, or are we having dinner?" Carter said, prodding me.

I snapped out of it and picked up the chair that had fallen behind me. "I'm sorry. I've got to run. I'm late, for, um, my date!"

I gave Mom and Dad a quick hug goodbye while rejecting Mom's several offers for a doggy bag.

"Congratulations," I said, quietly to my brother as I hugged him tight. I didn't have to agree with him to show him loving support. But it wasn't beneath me to tell him what I really thought when the time was right. But, tonight was not the night for honesty. I said my goodbyes, and I left with my burden. Only this time, it was heavier than when I came in.

I slammed my truck door closed. My eyes unfocused on the dashboard. That was a disaster! I failed my first real attempt at telling my family. And to be honest, it was most likely my last too.

I started the truck and made my way home, but not before swinging by the Red Brick Diner. Or as my brother called it, Red Ricks. I drove through the parking lot slowly as I tried to get a glimpse through the windows. There were about half a dozen customers, and I had no idea if any of them were Easton.

I sighed. I didn't know what I was thinking. I decided to go home because walking into the diner and ordering pie to go was too embarrassing. As soon as I made the call, though, loneliness crept in like a cold draft. I tried to push it out of my head by turning on the music, but then I remembered why it was off in the first place. The love song made me think about how I'd never given myself the chance to fall in love. And now, I would never know what it felt like. I didn't know how to help myself, but I wasn't ready to give up just yet. Yeti was waiting for me at home, and she would brighten my day with her big black doe eyes and wagging nub of a tail. She always did.

As I fumbled for my keys, Yeti scraped on the other side of the door. She was excited to shower me with love. Take my pain away. I was ready for it too. I opened the door, and she came bashing into me. I dropped my bag and kneeled, giving her face a vigorous rub.

Small bits of tan tattered cloth caught the corner of my vision. I lifted my head above Yeti to find countless pieces of chewed leopard leather all over the floor. The tiny ounce of pleasure my dog gave me quickly vanished. I stood up slowly and walked over to the first rogue leopard spot. It was still wet.

They were the first pair of brand-name high heels I'd ever bought, not even a week ago. I turned around to scold Yeti. Unleash all of my anger and frustrations about the impossible unfairness of this life! But she was cowering by the front door. If she had a longer tail, it would've tucked between her legs. I looked back at the mess on the floor. My fingernails were deep in my palms. There was no one to be angry with but myself. I guess I didn't have a purpose for shoes that would last me years anyway.

My bed was as cold and lonely as my heart, and slipping my legs under the blanket was just as miserable as hearing myself think. If there were a way I could shut it off, I would.

The walls of my bedroom seemed to enclose on me. I felt my heartrate pick up, and I knew I was on the verge of a panic attack. I was barely holding myself together. I scrunched my eyes closed as I thought about Easton's shoes hanging over the bridge. I didn't know his story, but I was beginning to empathize with him. Was it possible that he needed a friend too? My breathing began to steady. I shook the homeless man from my thoughts. It was weird I had even let him occupy this much of my mind in the first place.

But when I realized that thinking of him made me feel less alone, I had no choice but to allow my mind to wander.

I reached over and turned off the light on my nightstand, and patted my bed. Yeti jumped up and made her way to the empty spot next to me. It was the space that should've been taken by a lover but wasn't—some day.

I tapped my pencil ferociously against my binder. My *closed* binder. My eyes uncrossed when I heard my name called aloud.

"Miss. Beck? Do you have anything to add?" Mr. Pillson asked.

Several students looked back at me, causing my stomach to drop. My hands stopped fidgeting as I straightened my back. I shook my head and opened my binder. I wrote Multimedia and Animation across the top of my page. I'd just finished dating the paper when I felt his eyes lingering on me.

Dawson was my kind of guy. The type of guy whose abs showed through his T-shirt. The type of guy who probably washed his car in his driveway on the weekends—shirtless. He did in my dreams, anyway. It was no surprise that this class held my lowest academic grade. I'd spent most of my time flirting with Dawson. I often tried to talk to him. Every day was *the* day I was going to be brave. But, just like all the other days before, I would psych myself out at the last minute, and bolt for the door leaving Dawson hanging back in the classroom.

I was a chicken that way. Never having a real boyfriend put certain pressures on a girl. I didn't flirt today, but I did hurry out of class. I couldn't strike up a conversation *now*.

I weaved in and out of the student body, up the stairs, and out of the classroom. It was my lunch break. I got a Diet Coke and a bag of Skittles from the vending machine. It wasn't the healthiest lunch available, but I no longer worried about my health. I had for nearly two decades now, and look where it got me. I took my loot to the tree I liked to sit under. Only this time, I passed it and walked to the parking lot. The ground was too saturated, and unless I wanted to look like I wet myself, I had to eat lunch in my truck.

I untwisted the Coke cap and took a swig. The carbonation danced in my mouth, and my eyes watered. It was one of my favorite feelings. *Sad* really. If you asked anyone else what their favorite feeling was, they would probably have a much different answer.

I watched a girl pass my truck wearing a skirt so short that she didn't have to bend over for me to see her underwear. I wrinkled my nose. Skittles exploded everywhere in the cab of my truck as I fumbled and the bag ripped open. My lap covered in the rainbow.

I skipped my next class, Principles of Design and Color, to eat Skittles off my floor mat. There was no point in me getting good grades anymore. I didn't even know why I came to school today in the first place. I mixed orange and red in my mouth as I took out a piece of paper and wrote.

Dear Easton . . .

I wrote several versions of my letter until the Skittles

were replaced with crumpled up rejection letters. I stared at my name and number on an otherwise blank piece of paper. At least it was to the point. He would have to appreciate that, given my lack of time left. I shrugged to nobody but myself and finished my Coke.

The thought of attending my last class was less than appealing. Giving in to my new irresponsible mindset, I started the engine. My focus was now set on three places. The New River Bridge. Red Brick Diner. And lastly, Fresh Grounds. If Easton was the least bit interested in seeing me again, there was a small chance he would be hanging out at one of the spots we had previously seen each other.

I passed the New River Bridge, but only let off the gas a little. There was no need to slow down to see that Easton wasn't there. No parked cars and no homeless man standing on the rails. I trudged forward. The crisp air seemed to buzz with electricity. Maybe it was my destiny, maybe it was static, but I had a good feeling about this.

I turned into the empty parking lot of the diner. This time, I decided to park and head inside. The doorbells jingled as I crossed the threshold, the letter in my hand. I walked up to the bar, scanning the booths for a slender build and pale face with messy hair, and the eyes that made me forget I was sick. My stomach dropped, and for the life of me, I didn't know why.

A waitress rounded the corner, wiping her hands on a dishtowel. I recognized those boobs. Sue. I caught myself mid-eye-roll and forced myself to be polite. Maybe she was in a better mood today.

"Hi! Um, Sue?" I waved my hand, and even though she

saw me, she kept walking. I scurried after her. "Sue?" My voice squeaked with the effort.

"I'll be right with you," Sue said and had the audacity to hold her finger up as if I were too dense to understand English. This time, I let my eyes do their thing. Sue busied herself behind the bar as I waited.

"Hi there! I knew you would be back!" Sue perked up so much that she looked like a different person altogether. Her whole face glowed. I scowled at her obvious distaste for me. I looked over my shoulder to see who the lucky customer was to have won the affections of Sue and her big bust, but I whipped my head back when I saw Easton closing in on me. My eyes bugged, and suddenly, I second-guessed the whole plan.

Easton placed his hands on the bar next to me. I slowly moved the letter in my hand to the inside of my jacket. I could feel him staring at me, but unlike Dawson from school, I needed something from Easton. I swallowed, refusing to look at him.

"Hello, Sue. How are you doing today?" Easton said, only quickly taking his eyes off of me. I peeked at him. His hair was the same mop of a mess, and he was wearing his wool coat—still not homeless. Why did I keep thinking this man was homeless?

"I'm doing better now that you're here, darling! What can I get you?" Sue whipped the dish towel over her shoulder.

"Ladies first," Easton gestured to me. My eyes met Sue's and her one raised eyebrow.

I swallowed again. "I'll have the pie. To go." It was even

more embarrassing than I'd imagined last night. "Please," I said just under my breath. I knew it didn't mean anything to her. Still, I had to say it for me.

When Sue turned away, I looked up at Easton. "You found me," I said, unsure of myself. My cheeks warm, and my forehead creased. Easton smiled and pulled out a blue vinyl barstool and sat. I followed his lead.

Sue slid a box across the counter and handed me a check. "And what can I get for you, sir?" She shimmied her shoulders, too excited to stand still. I sat in front of the to-go container awkwardly.

"I'll have the same. It looks delicious. Did you make it yourself?" Easton asked.

"I did! How did you know that?" Sue placed her hand on her hip.

"Oh, just a hunch!" Easton leaned over the bar. "Between you and me, I don't think Bill is much of a baker!" Easton said, in a hushed voice, and Sue squealed. She looked back into the kitchen at who I presumed was Bill and giggled as she swatted the air.

I couldn't believe Easton put the time and effort into making her so happy. It probably wasn't much work on his side, but it sure did make her day. I wanted to be like him. I wanted to make someone's day, too. Not Sue's, though.

CHAPTER 6

Sue placed a warm slice of blackberry pie in front of Easton, complete with a napkin and fork. I looked down at my cold pie inside of its to-go box.

"Can I have a fork, please?" I asked Sue. I forced a smile, but she never looked to see it. I suppose it was too late to ask for a plate.

"Funny how we keep running into each other," I said, knowing very well I came to the Red Brick Diner looking for him. I wondered if he was here doing the same. Sue placed a fork in front of me, and I smiled, but I didn't look to confirm my rejection. There was only so much a girl could take.

"Maybe it's fate," Easton said.

At first, I worried he might like me, and I was giving him the wrong impression, but then I remembered that he was the only one that knew my existence was temporary. Why would anyone want to get involved with that baggage? And if he were crazy enough to actually want me in my broken state, it was kind of like having a get out of jail free card. There were too many excuses to pick from.

"Maybe," I said, still contemplating my stance.

"Do you come here often?" Easton asked and took a bite of pie.

I ripped my box so the edges would lay flat like a plate. "I . . . don't, really. I just wanted something sweet." I shrugged.

I was still reeling from the soda and Skittles I ate off my floorboards. I frowned at the thought of my dishonesty. Was I ever going to tell the truth again? I slumped as I continued to disappoint myself.

"Actually, I came here looking for you." I took a bite of the pie and I tried to build the courage to keep going.

"You came here looking for me?" Easton asked, his eyebrows lifting. I feared his surprise came from me telling the truth and not that I was looking for him.

I pushed away the pie that I never wanted in the first place and turned my full attention to Easton. It was time to be honest. I owed that to myself.

"I tried to tell my parents, but it didn't go so well. They were so happy that I couldn't bring myself to tell them the truth. I don't think I'm ready to tell them, and I'm not sure I ever will be. Do you think that makes me a bad person?" I looked down at my feet, afraid of what his eyes might say.

Easton took a moment to think. I could hear it in his deep sigh. "No," he said in a tone too high to convince me that he was telling the truth. I peeked up at him. "I mean, it's your life. You get to live the way you want to, and that's the beauty of it, right? It doesn't make you bad or good to live the way you desire to," Easton said as he dug himself out of his hole. It worked, though. The profound guilt about my decision not to tell my family began to lift. The corners of my lips lifted as I nodded my head, accepting his point of view.

"Thank you for that. You've somehow managed to put my mind at ease. That's not an easy task. Especially not these days," I said.

"You don't have to thank me. I'm happy to help." Easton took his last bite and pushed his plate away. "Now, you said you were looking for me?"

Was my update not enough of a reason? I raked my mind for other lies. I couldn't tell him I needed him to be my fake boyfriend. It was absurd and embarrassing, and that was just the beginning. I pulled out the note from inside my jacket. It was just my name and number, thank God.

"I wanted to give this to you." I slid him the note on top of the bar.

His face bent with curiosity, and he opened the folded paper.

"You know, just in case you needed anything." I tried to make it sound like it was for him and not me. I don't know why that was my first instinct, but it was. I hated the way I felt like I couldn't simply ask for help. Sue gathered Easton's plate and handed him the check.

"OK, thanks for this." Easton smiled and put the note in his back pocket before turning his attention towards his check.

I'm not sure if he was calling my bluff or not, but I felt the panic creep in. Was that it? That couldn't be it!

"Um, well like, maybe you want to hang out or something? You know if that was the case, you could call me too." I waved my hand in the air as if it were nothing. But in all honesty, he was the only one keeping me sane, and I needed him for my mental health. I also needed him not to blow my whole boyfriend story.

Easton slammed the pen down on his check and turned to me. "You don't have time for games," he said matter-of-factly. His tone was sharp, his words cutting.

I looked away from his glacier blue eyes. It hurt to hear. I felt like Yeti cowering in the admission of guilt. He was right. He was *always* right.

"If you tell me that the number is for me to call if *I* need *you*, I'm not calling. Like I told you before, I'm fine. Would you mind telling me why you really came here looking for me? And what this number is really about?" Easton lowered his head to try to make eye contact with me. Reluctantly, I let him.

"You're right. I'm sorry. I don't know why I said that. The number isn't for you. It's for me. I need a friend right now"—my eyes began to well up—"and you're the only one who understands me . . . as odd as that is, given the fact that you're a total stranger to me. I just feel *really* alone." A single tear dripped down my cheek, and I wiped it away as quickly as it came. I tilted my head back and blinked several times, urging the tears to stop their madness.

"I would really appreciate it if I could just call you sometime or if we could hang out. That's all." I lowered my head to find Easton with an apologetic look on his face. My confession was all he wanted. Not the part that brought me to tears.

"There, was that so hard?" Easton asked and handed me his napkin.

I rolled my eyes. Damn boy. I blotted the corner of my eyes, and Easton chuckled at my theatrics.

"Look, I value honesty. If you want to be my friend, you have to be honest." Easton held out his hand.

I looked up into his eyes. They were full of sincerity. I reached out and grabbed his hand. It was warm and strong. My dad always told me that a firm handshake was important in a man. He would like Easton.

"Deal," I said, ignoring my omission of truth. Eventually, I would tell him when he wasn't a stranger, and I was ready to laugh about the lie I told my family.

We both stood and tucked in our barstools. Easton said goodbye to Sue, and I waited while he made her smile one last time. We made our way out of the diner and through the parking lot. Easton walked me to my truck. I opened my door but stopped before getting inside. The cold air wrapped around my neck, and I zipped my jacket as high as it would go.

"So, when are we going to hang out, friend?" Easton asked me, and a genuine smile spread across my face. It felt good to have a friend.

A black sedan pulled into the parking lot and caught my eye. I peered over Easton's shoulder. Heat washed over my cheeks as I realized that it was my mom. Again. My eyes grew wide, causing Easton to look behind him. *No. No. No . . .*

The clacking of my mom's shoes became louder. Easton was thrilled and took full enjoyment in my discomfort. He was probably the only person that would enjoy my embarrassment in my condition. And perhaps, it was the very reason I liked him. *Liked him?*

"Mrs. Beck! How wonderful to see you again. How has your day been?"

I prayed that she wouldn't say anything incriminating. But I knew my mother, and I knew that wasn't going to be the case.

"Easton! Hello again!" Mom laughed as she grabbed at his arm. "Dear, I just saw your truck as I was driving to the market and I thought . . . don't you have school today?" Mom looked down at her watch.

Clover was a small town. If my red truck was in a parking lot, every local in this town knew I was inside; and if Mom was driving to the supermarket and I was playing hooky, I was sure to be discovered. I thought this was frustrating when I was in high school, but it was even worse now that I was an adult.

"My teacher let us out early," I said, my eyes shifting between the two of them.

"Ohhh. OK. So, how was dinner last night?" Mom looked at Easton, then me.

Shit!

"Oh, yeah, we had fun. It was a good night." I nodded my head. Easton didn't have to know who "we" was, right? It could have been a girl's night out for all he knew.

"Well, I won't keep you two. Easton, I do hope you will come over for dinner soon?" Mom grabbed at Easton's arm again, and I sucked in a sharp breath.

"It's a date!" Easton said, smiling first at my mom and then me. Her face lit up.

All three of us stood in a silent web of lies until Easton broke the ice. "Well, I'll see you tonight then?" He raised his eyebrows at me and cocked his head to the side.

Tonight?

"Yes!" I said in absolute confusion.

Easton placed his hand over mine as I held onto my door and leaned down nearly two inches from my face. My stomach dropped as he closed his eyes and puckered his lips. My eyes grew wide with alarm. *What was he doing!?*

My mom lit up like a Christmas tree. I felt the pressure of her watching us and him waiting on me, and the seconds ticking by in slow motion. How long was he going to wait like a fool? I instantaneously decided to put him out of his misery. I rose up on my toes to close the inches between us and our lips met. I closed my eyes briefly before pulling away—as my stomach did somersaults.

Upon opening my eyes, Easton's smirk said it all. He got me. He got me good. Mom clapped. I was several shades of mortified.

The two of them turned to walk away. "I told you, you're her first boyfriend ever! So, she might come across a little timid . . ." Her voice faded into the distance.

I stood at my truck with my jaw dropped as I put the pieces together. "How wonderful to see you *again*." I assumed *again* was the first time they met, but clearly, it was not. I immediately regretted promising Easton a friendship built on trust. He had already known I was lying. He made me pay for my sins with a kiss. I brought my fingertips to my lips. I guess it could have been worse.

My mom walked into the diner, and Easton started his engine. I didn't know much about cars, but I knew that he definitely wasn't living rough. He pulled up next to me in his silver BMW and rolled down the tinted window.

"Hunters. 6:00 PM. Tonight," he said, pulling away before I could protest. My face contorted as I struggled to make out my emotions. I was irritated, deceived, angry . . . impressed, captivated, and excited.

CHAPTER 7

Red lace was too sexy. It wasn't a *real* date. Easton knew enough to know it was all for show. The dinner was more of a business transaction than anything else. What would I have to pay for a fake boyfriend? What did non-homeless Easton Green want?

My attention snapped back to the red lace. *No. I'll never wear that again.* I grabbed a sheer button-down blouse instead. The black top would have looked killer with my leopard heels. I bit my lip, thinking about the chewed-up shoes I never had the chance to wear. Alternatively, I slipped black boots over my jeans. They were weather appropriate at least. I threw on a necklace and grabbed my jacket before heading out the door. I was going to be early, but that's the way I liked it.

"Hello, I'm meeting somebody here at six," I informed the hostess. She checked her clipboard. I don't know how she could read it in this lighting. The ambiance was dark and romantic. Much too dark to read handwriting.

"You must be Everly?" the hostess said. I guess that her eyes had adjusted.

I smiled and nodded.

"Right this way." She turned and walked away.

I followed her through the small and intimate steakhouse. It was the only one in Clover. Every date happened here, and everyone knew who was seeing who. I spotted my dentist and his wife in the corner and pretended I didn't see them. My stomach dropped when we rounded the corner, and Easton came into my view. I don't know why I felt nervous. It was stupid, really.

Easton stood when I approached the table. He cleaned up nice. He was wearing a black-collared shirt and a smile. His hair styled with gel.

I received the menu from the hostess and took my seat. I thought about our kiss in the parking lot, and butterflies stirred in my stomach. I wouldn't say I liked Easton, but maybe I liked the way I felt around him.

"You look nice," I said before hiding behind my menu. The dim, romantic lighting was forgiving in the way he could no longer see my blushing cheeks and flushed chest.

"As do you," Easton said.

I glanced over the menu without reading. I had my order memorized since I was a kid. I never got anything but the chicken breast, mashed potatoes, and veggies. Mostly I filled up on the hot squaw bread and butter that came out as an appetizer. I slowly lowered my menu to take a peek at the boy across from me. I needed to get a read on the situation. His hair, slowly . . . his forehead . . . *dammit!* He was staring right at me! His hands folded on top of his menu. Confidence would be an understatement.

"OK, look! I told my family I had a boyfriend . . . it was my *mom* who told everyone else it was the 'cute boy from the coffee shop'" I curled my fingers into air quotes.

Easton's eyebrows lifted. "Cute boy?" he asked, clinging to the adjective.

Dear God! I'm either lying through my teeth or shooting myself in the foot. I stared at Easton blankly. I couldn't tell him that he wasn't my type! That his lack of abs left me with little to fantasize about! That would be . . . *evil.* I swallowed hard, and he just smirked back at me. Maybe I would go to hell.

"I'm sorry. This was a bad idea!" I said, starting to fidget for my purse.

"No! Don't go!" Easton pleaded, and my body stilled. "We don't have to be anything you don't want. I'm happy being your friend if that's what you need." He reached his hand out and placed it on mine.

I looked down at his hand. Warm on top of mine. I didn't know what to say. I didn't know what I wanted. I only knew that my pathetic life was better with him in it. I nodded and set my purse down. When Easton pulled his hand back, I wished that he hadn't.

"And I'm sorry I kissed you. I know I put you on the spot. It was only a joke," Easton said. I knew it was to get back at me, but calling it a joke hurt a little. I felt the ebb and flow between us, like an invisible string attaching us together. He pulls back, and I lean in.

"No, I know. That's OK. I know you were just getting

back at me. I'm sorry I hid the fake relationship thing from you. I . . . never thought you would find out," I confessed. The honesty, as blunt as it was, felt good.

Easton laughed. "So, you're only sorry because you got caught?" he asked.

Now it was my turn to laugh. I thought about it. He was right as usual. "Yes!" I laughed again. It felt nice to laugh. Refreshing.

"My name is Kyle, and I'll be your waiter today. Can I get you started with a drink?" The waiter asked with his hands tucked behind his back.

"I'll have the red blend, please," I said.

"Make that two."

Now was my chance. I was going to make someone's day the way Easton had. I scanned the waiter for something to compliment him on. He looked . . . entirely average! *Just pick anything . . .*

"I like your shirt!" I blurted out.

The waiter frowned briefly before running his hand over a missing button. He faked a smile before dashing away.

"Oh, no!" My mouth gaped as I stared at Easton in disbelief. "I was just trying to say something nice, and he thinks I was sarcastic!" My eyes bulged with worry. I lowered my head to my palm.

"Oh, that's what you were doing?" Easton looked behind him, checking for the waiter. "Nooo, I don't think he was offended." It was his turn to fib.

"You're lying to me! We can't be friends unless we're honest with each other! You made a deal!" I accused him, finger-pointing and all.

"*I* made a deal that *you* couldn't lie!" Easton corrected me.

Was that how it went? I struggled to remember anything but the kiss.

"OK, from now on, nobody lies. Ever!" I said, and I meant it. I thrust my hand across the table for another handshake deal.

Easton hesitated. He swallowed and stared at my hand without making an advance. "What's wrong?" I asked him.

"Nothing," he said in an unconvincing tone before shaking my hand. It didn't go without notice that his once firm handshake had wilted. No longer the firm and confident dealmaker from the diner. I scowled. He's hiding something already. But I wasn't angry with him. I knew what it was like to have secrets. To be buried in shame and embarrassment.

Kyle placed two red wine blends down on our table, and I couldn't help but look at the missing button from his shirt. He took our order while nervously pulling at his clothes. There was a special place in hell for me.

Easton raised his glass. "To a friendship built on your honesty," he said.

I laughed. "Wait, you didn't think that would actually work, did you?" I asked through my amusement.

"To a friendship built on honesty," Easton corrected himself.

We tapped our glasses together and took a sip of wine. It was good—the perfect blend of sweet and cherry tart. I placed my glass down on the table with a sense of renewed life. I no longer felt alone. I effortlessly connected with

Easton as long as I took off my armor of lies. I could do it for him . . . for me. Whatever it was, I liked it.

"How are you doing? Where's your mind at?" Easton asked.

"My mind?" It was pretty good until he asked. "Um, I'm . . . well, this helps." I gestured to him across the table. "You're a decent distraction. When I'm with you, I find myself forgetting that my life's imploding." I sucked in a shaky breath. It was unlike me to be so honest about my feelings. But I was trying.

"I *can* help distract you," Easton agreed.

My eyebrows furrowed. It's what I wanted to hear, so why was I upset? I played with my wine glass.

"Why are you doing this?" I asked, not wanting to know the truth.

Easton appeared to be caught off guard. He nodded, taking in my frustration along with a leisurely sip of wine. My irritation grew.

"Don't get caught up in your self-pity. You're going to get that from everyone else in your life, but you won't get it from me." He looked around the restaurant before leaning in. He spoke low and rushed. "I'm not your friend because you're dying. I'm your friend because I happen to like you. You're different. You're in an odd situation. And I enjoy being around you and your thoughts, emotions, and actions. Don't get me wrong. I'm just as selfish as anyone else out there, but I'm not doing this for a good conscience. I'm doing it out of my own damn self-interest. Don't you forget it!" Easton leaned back in his seat as Kyle brought us our food.

Frozen in shock, I needed a moment to take it all in. Buttered garlic swirled under my nose, and despite my distaste for the lecture, my mouth began to water.

I *didn't* want pity, and his brutal honesty is what I had just asked for, so I couldn't fault him for it.

"Are you mad at me?" I asked, trying to understand my ever-changing emotions.

"Mad? I'm not mad at you. You just need to hear the truth. Sometimes it hurts a little, but I've just vowed to be honest with you, so my relationship with you will be very different from my relationship with Sue at the diner. Does that make sense?" Easton asked as he tore apart his steak.

"You mean you don't think Sue has the prettiest eyes?" A small smile crept across my face as I began to forgive my new friend for snapping at me. Yes, the truth hurt, but the thought of not having him at all hurt more. Easton's eyes grew large, and his smile said what he did not.

"Look. This thing between you and I . . . it's different, right?" Easton motioned between us with his fork.

"Yes," I admitted.

"You don't have time for games, right?" he continued.

"No," I said, totally drawn in. I think I liked where this was going.

"So, let's just lay it all out on the table? Yes?" He nodded, willing me to do the same.

"Yes!" I said enthusiastically.

"You need a fake boyfriend to keep your parents in the dark because you're a coward and can't tell them the truth about your diagnosis," he said as I nodded greedily. It was all out in the raw open air, and I felt liberated.

"You're too afraid of pity, so you haven't told any of your friends. You're lonely beyond belief, and you need company." A smile spread across his face. "*My* company," he said.

I continued to agree.

"So, let's just do the damn thing! Let's be as real and as greedy as we need to be. And let's get you through the next several months." The candle's flame danced in Easton's eyes.

"Yes! Can we do that, please?" I asked. It was more than I ever knew I wanted. Who knew the truth could be so freeing?

Easton slammed his palm down on the table and our silverware clamored. "Yes!" he said—seemingly louder than he'd anticipated. He hunched and looked around nervously.

I felt electric. More alive than I had in a long time.

"OK, we've got to get to work! Hold on." Easton got up from the table and walked away. Where was he going? I waited impatiently, still too excited to eat.

Easton returned with a take-out menu and a pen. "OK, tell me all the things you've wanted to do in your life but haven't yet." Easton held the pen to the paper.

"Like a bucket list?" I asked.

"Yeah, yeah, like a bucket list. Do you have one?" he asked, staring into my eyes.

"No. I mean, not yet!" I said.

"That's what I like to hear!" Easton shook his pen at me, and I smiled, wanting nothing more in that moment than to be under his praise.

"Um . . . I've never seen the northern lights!" I said, rushed, and Easton scribbled it down.

"I've never bungee jumped! I've never gone camping! Or gotten a tattoo." It was all just spilling out.

Easton stopped writing and peeked up at me. "Wait, these are things that you *want* to do, not just stuff you've never done," he clarified, his forehead creased as he looked up at me with those eyes.

"I know!" I said, just as confused as he was.

"Nobody *wants* to go camping," he said.

I laughed aloud. "I do! I want to sleep under the stars and roast marshmallows!" I nodded my head as he shook his in disagreement.

"That's not—"

"Just write it down!" I said.

"OK," he muttered and began to write again. Our food was starting to get cold, but neither one of us paid it any mind.

"I want to ride a horse on the beach. I want to skinny dip . . . or go streaking! I want to crash a wedding!"

The word wedding stung as soon as it left my mouth. The fun had been replaced by an ache in my chest. My eyes settled on the dancing flame of the scentless candle on our table.

"I'll never get married, or dance at my wedding. I'll never fall in love . . ." The realization that my bucket list was impossible to fill was devastating. I sank in my seat. My throat burned as I held back my tears.

Easton continued to write, and I drowned myself in wine, proceeding to flag our waiter over to ask for a refill.

"Hey, weddings are overrated anyway." Easton shrugged, careful not to mention that falling in love was . . . totally worth it. But I could read between the lines, and I wondered what epic love story he had already experienced or would in his long life.

"Yeah, totally overrated." I shook away my tears. "Hey! We have to make your bucket list too," I said, trying to sound optimistic. I reached my hand across the table for my turn with the menu and pen.

Easton froze. He didn't like the idea as much as I did. "We don't have to do that. Let's just focus on you," he said and looked back to the menu.

"No! Come on. Don't be like that!" I protested and flapped my hand, begging for the menu.

"I've done a lot of stuff already; there's not much more for me to do," Easton said and batted my hand away.

I wouldn't accept his nonsense. "You're my age. What, like twenty-two, twenty-five? How have you done everything you want to do already?" I shook my head, not believing my "honest" friend.

Easton rolled his eyes before caving. He slid me the pen and menu. I silently cheered and took them from him. I flipped the menu over and wrote his name at the top.

"Ready!" I said.

"I've never crashed a wedding with you . . . I've never gone camping with you," Easton started in a slow and soothing voice.

My heart sank. "I've never danced at your wedding," he said, and my tears threatened to spill over again.

I didn't write anything on the menu. I just nodded and

gazed into his eyes. We shared a moment of understanding. Neither one of us needed to say what we felt to know that it was kind, compassionate, and completely mutual. I didn't know his reasons for needing our friendship, but I knew the desire was shared.

CHAPTER 8

$\mathcal{I}$'ll take it to go, please," I said to our waiter. Having only eaten a couple of bites, there was a possibility of me getting hungry later tonight. Easton read me his number as I entered the digits in my phone.

"You have to promise to call me if you need anything," he said with raised eyebrows.

"I promise. You too." I said.

"Any time of day or night, OK?"

I nodded my head. "I promise I'll call you," I said and smiled. "You too! This goes both ways." I pointed my finger at him in a flirtatious manner. He enjoyed it.

The waiter brought us our check, and I considered a way to right my wrong about the missing button on his shirt but ultimately decided I had dug a hole I couldn't climb out of. Easton paid, and I thanked him. I took the last sip of my wine before standing up and grabbing my purse. Where were all of the people? The restaurant was nearly empty. I checked my watch, it was almost 10:00 p.m.

"We've been here for four hours!?" I asked Easton, bewildered.

He checked the time on his phone and seemed to be surprised too. "Really?" he looked at me like someone was playing a trick on us, and I laughed. He placed his hand between my shoulder blades as we walked out of the restaurant. It was a friendly gesture, but it still made me blush, just a little.

I paused momentarily when I recognized someone I knew at the bar. Hope. I lifted onto my tippytoes, trying to get a look at the guy she was with. I was just like everyone else in Clover. Nosey.

"Someone you know?" Easton asked, looking at the couple at the bar.

"Yeah, that's Hope." I looked back at Easton as he took her in.

She was the girl next door. Not literally, but physically. She was beautiful, but most men looked it over, including my brother. He was too blind to see that she had feelings for him. Hope was his perfect match, and by the looks of it, she had started dating again. I frowned and kept walking.

"She's the girl I wanted my brother to marry, but he's too dense to see that she's the total package. Now, he's marrying some bimbo." I filled Easton in as our walk slowed to a crawl. He opened the door for me, and the cold air nipped at my nose.

"A bimbo! Is that right?" Easton laughed. "I haven't heard that one in a while."

I rolled my eyes at him. Chloe didn't appear to have brains—just a pretty exterior. I scowled when I realized that

I had always gone for the same type. Perhaps it ran in the family.

"She's the dating type, not the marrying type if you get my drift," I said as I dug for my keys in my purse.

"Got it. So what's the deal with Hope then?" Easton asked, his hands tucked deep into his pockets.

"Well, our families used to be good friends when we were younger. They lived in the neighborhood. She always had a crush on my brother. He thought she had cooties. When they were fresh out of high school, they worked together at the supermarket. They spent all their breaks together and became fast friends. It was clear that she never lost feelings for him, but my brother never took the bait. I don't know why." I shrugged, looking back into Hunters' windows, but they were too dark to see inside.

"Maybe, it wasn't meant to be." Easton said.

I shrugged, not yet convinced. "I had a great night. Thank you." It was the most comfortable truth of the night.

Easton smiled back at me. "Thank you for not blowing me off. I thought there was a chance after my stunt in the parking lot today!" He laughed and looked down at his feet.

My stomach lurched at the mention of our kiss. I shoved him playfully.

"I'll get you for that. Someday," I promised him. I got into my truck and started the engine. Easton stayed by my door side. I rolled my window down a notch.

"Don't forget to call if you need me!" he reminded me.

I lifted my phone and gave it a shake. Then, I pulled out

of the parking spot and made my way home with an empty belly and a full heart.

Easton's friendship was enough to keep the terrors away that night. My house was empty, but my mind was occupied. The bed was cold but not unbearable. And I was dying . . . but not tonight.

My alarm blared, waking me again. It was the fourth time I'd hit snooze, and each time I'd fallen fast asleep. I finally turned the alarm off altogether and rolled over. Not today. Work was the least of my concerns. Yeti rolled onto her back, wiggling and scratching, causing the bed to shake and my eyes to open. The more conscious I became, the more guilty I felt. Lindsay would be expecting me. I couldn't let her down. I groaned as I threw off the covers. I should just quit. Both school and work. I contemplated the idea as I got dressed and brushed my teeth. Maybe I wasn't ready to have full days of loneliness, but at some point, I wouldn't have another choice.

The silent drive to work got me thinking of my date last night. I'd be lying if I said I'd thought of anything else. A simple drive through Clover, and the diner lifted my spirits. Passing Hunters was equally uplifting. And Fresh Grounds made me flush with embarrassment when I thought of Easton warming up to my mom. A small pang of guilt seeped into my mind as I put my truck into park. Was I using Easton?

When I walked into Fresh Grounds, I was pleased to see

Greg's camel jacket in line. The smell of coffee and all things pastry told me I'd made the right decision coming in to work. I whispered my order to Lindsay before checking into my cash register.

"Greg, I can help you over here." I waved him over. "How are you doing today?" I asked as I started putting in his order.

"I'm good. I'm good. I'll have the regular," he said, pulling out his wallet.

"And how is Carol?" I asked.

"She's good. She's all wrapped up in this book where a boy freezes himself. He wakes up twenty years later and falls in love. She says it's captivating but won't tell me the ending. Says I have to read it myself. She knows I don't read that stuff." Greg batted his hand across the air.

I laughed and took his money. "Maybe you would like it?"

"Me? No . . . I don't want to read about love. That's for you girls!" Greg shook his head as if I were crazy.

I giggled. "Your order will be right out."

"Thanks, Beck."

The line was small today. I grabbed my latte from Lindsay, and we chatted as I practiced making a heart out of foam.

"Why didn't you tell me you had a boyfriend!?" Lindsay hissed like the milk steamer.

My cheeks flushed, and for a moment, I contemplated which side of the truth she would fall on.

"He's *not* my boyfriend!" *Shit.* Wrong side.

"He's not? Because your mom came in here yesterday," Lindsay started.

"I just said that to her so I could get her off my back! Carter's engaged now, and my mom has been riding me about never having a boyfriend. She brings it up all the time." This part was true. She did bring it up whenever she could. "He's just a friend," I said, turning my latte heart into a cloud. I was surprised by how the last part was the part that made me feel guilty. He was a friend, but in a lot of ways, he was more than that, too.

"Oh shit! It was so bad that you had to make up a boyfriend?" Lindsay laughed hard enough to fold in half and slap her hand on the bar several times.

I grabbed Greg's coffees and set them on the ledge. "Greg, your order is ready!" I called out to him.

"So wait, wait . . . does that guy know? Because your mom sat down with him for a *while*! Lord knows what she told him!" Lindsay blotted her left eye with the back of her hand.

"I mean, yeah, I had to tell him." I couldn't help but smirk. Her laugh was so over the top, it finally got to me.

"Actually, I had dinner with him last night. I had to tell him the whole thing. It was utterly embarrassing!" Among other things . . .

"Thanks, Greg! Tell Carol to enjoy that book!" I waved goodbye.

"I will!" Greg held up his coffees.

Lindsay threw her hand on her hip. "No!" Her mouth opened into an elongated O.

I nodded.

"How did you even meet this guy?" Lindsay prodded.

I pictured the torrential downpour of the storm and Easton's wet hair plastered to the side of his face, his body shivering. He was a different person at that moment. I hadn't seen that guy since the bridge.

"School," I said, but it came out sounding more like a question than a statement. I was relieved when I heard customers walk in. I thought it would end there, but it didn't. Lindsay poked and prodded about Easton all day. I grew tired of dodging her questions, and I knew I wouldn't be able to keep my lies in order.

It was almost time for me to get off work when I got a text from Easton. I pulled my phone out of my back pocket and smiled instantly when I saw his name.

Easton: What are you doing?

I typed as fast as I could.

Me: Working.

I waited for his reply, careful not to let Lindsay see.

Easton: I'll be there in ten.

My eyes widened, and a wave of heat blanketed my back as I felt my cheeks pinken. I tucked my phone in my pocket and raked my fingers through my hair, trying to comb out a day's work.

"You OK?" Lindsay asked. She was oddly perceptive.

"Yeah!" I furrowed my brows . . . because why *wouldn't* I be OK?

How would she react when Easton came in? I hoped she wouldn't say anything.

Every time the door opened, I jumped, and Lindsay observed my sudden shift in mood.

When Easton finally walked through the doors, my stomach dropped. I was nervous all over again. Every time was like the *first* time.

"Oh! Oh!" Lindsay started, slapping my hip beneath the countertop.

"Shhh!" I hissed back at her. Easton saw the shuffled exchange between us, and it caused a stifled grin to appear on his face.

"You must be the infamous Easton?" Lindsay asked.

Shit! Here we go!

"Hi!" I said, taking off my apron and walking out from behind the bar to convey that this was not a three-way conversation.

"I have a proposition for you," Easton said into my ear as we walked into the corner of the coffee shop that resembled a used book store.

"A proposition?" I asked. I didn't know what it was, but he didn't need to say any more. I was in.

"Do you have plans tonight?" Easton's face lit up while he waited for my answer.

"Tonight? Um, no . . ." I was already planning what to wear in my head.

"OK, I'll pick you up at eight?" he asked, just as excited as I was.

I nodded. "Sure, I'll text you my address," I said, still unsure of what I was getting myself into.

Easton's grin widened as he started to step back towards the door.

"Wait, what do I wear?" I perked up.

"A dress." Easton gave me one last smirk before turning around.

Oh, no! Not a dress! I stood in the corner of the coffee shop, scowling. I knew I didn't have a dress. I hadn't worn one since prom, and I was pretty sure that when he said *dress*, he didn't mean a fuchsia floor-length gown. I was so distraught I didn't hear Lindsay when she came up behind me.

"Did you just break up with your fake boyfriend? Cause you look knocked sideways," she said," trying to read my face.

I closed my mouth and looked at her square in the eyes.

"Do you have a dress I could borrow?" I searched her eyes for the *yes* I so desperately needed.

"Um, yeah. I have a few dresses?" she started.

"Thank you! Oh my God, thank you!" I gave her a quick hug.

"What's going on?" Lindsay asked as we made our way back behind the counter.

"I have a date!" I shrugged and slipped my apron back on for the last ten minutes I had on my shift.

"Like, a *real* one?" Lindsay's face was lined with confusion.

I cracked. My shoulders dropped, and my back slouched. "I don't know!!! I don't know!" my voice came out whiny and annoying. I was no better than a toddler throwing a fit for candy at the supermarket. There were so many feelings and lies; I couldn't possibly keep track of them all. I didn't know if it was a fake date or a real one—if we were friends or something more. And if it hadn't been for the stupid kiss that I continued to lose my stomach over, I might just have a grasp on this thing. But as for right now, all I knew was that I looked hideous in dresses.

"It's OK!" Lindsay patted my arm. "Look, come over after work, and we'll try on some dresses, OK?" Lindsay looked at her watch. "The next shift should be here any second." And as soon as she said it, Amy walked in the door. "See?" Lindsay nodded, and I felt my panic begin to dissipate.

I sat on Lindsay's unmade bed while she rummaged through her closet. Clothes littered her floor, presumably dirty. Her cat took a liking to me today, but when it jumped onto my lap, all I could think about was its paws digging through its litter box. By the smell of it, the thing was nearby.

"So, I have this one that might be a little too big for you in the boobs, but you can try it on." She held out a teal satin dress that looked like the boobs were already inside. I nodded. This was going to be a disaster.

"There's this one that I wore to my sister-in-law's baby shower. It's more forgiving in the chest because you can tighten the straps." Lindsay threw a lacy floral dress on her bed. I nodded again, praying there was more.

"Oh! And there's this one, but it's kind of boring." She held a grey turtleneck T-shirt dress by her side. "And you have *no* idea what you're going to be doing tonight?" she asked for the third time.

"No! I have no freaking clue! It's seriously stressing me out!" I placed my palm against my forehead. I jiggled my legs so the cat would jump off me. I couldn't take the feces feet any longer.

"Well, don't do that, um . . ." Lindsay bit her lip, a habit she'd gotten from me. "I could . . . take a peek in my sister's closet?"

I sat straight up. "Really?" I asked with rising hope.

"Yeah, I mean, she usually comes home on the weekends, but I don't think she would notice. Here, I'll see what I can find. Be right back!" Lindsay scurried out of her room, and I gave a sigh of relief. I studied her Blake Shelton posters on her wall while I waited.

Lindsay was overly excited when she returned with what she thought was the perfect match. "Look what I found!" Lindsay shimmied her shoulders as she held out a baby blue slip dress. Simple, like me.

"Yes! Oh my God, thank you!" I jumped up and took the dress from her.

"Yeah, just bring it back soon, so I can pop it back in her closet, OK?" she asked.

"Absolutely! Thank you!" I hugged her briefly before getting on my way.

CHAPTER 9

I jumped when Easton knocked on my door. Even Yeti was surprised. She leaped from her bed, bounded across the small living room, and raced to the front door, barking all the way. She was ferocious when she needed to be. I held her by the collar as I opened the door. Easton was handsome in his navy suit, his top two buttons undone. I caught his eye for a split second before Yeti's strength overpowered mine; she pushed the door open and escaped from my grasp.

Lucky for Easton, Yeti was full. But what surprised me more than her lack of aggression was the fact that she wagged her nub tail in excitement. Small whimpers escaped her as if seeing an old friend. I'd never seen her act like that.

I watched Easton win the heart of Yeti in an instant, and I wondered if he'd done the same to me when I lost my stomach. I pushed away my nerves and called Yeti into the house.

"Sorry!" I said, noting the smudge of slobber on Easton's pants.

"Don't be. I love dogs. What's his name?" Easton asked.

"*Her* name is Yeti," I said with my back to Easton as I locked my door.

His proximity did weird things to my insides as I took in the smell of his woody, sensual cologne. I sucked in a quick and shallow breath of air when I spun around to find Easton much closer than I expected. I smiled nervously and tucked my hair behind my ear, trapped between him and my locked door.

"You look beautiful tonight," Easton said slow and calm.

My heart pounded in my chest. A part of me couldn't take the closeness and all of the emotions that came with it. Another, albeit a small part, wanted to see what would happen if we lingered like this a little while longer.

Only after sensing my nervousness did he take a step back and say, "Welp, we better get a move on it! Can't be late!" He walked to his car and opened the passenger's door for me. It was when he pulled back that I saw what I truly wanted.

So gentlemanly of him to open my door. This *was* a date then. It felt like a date. My eyes darted around the car, searching for the answers to my indecisiveness. I felt like a hamster on a wheel, running as fast as my legs could take me . . . in no particular direction and with no end in sight.

"Where are we going?" I asked, my forehead still creased with my unsettled feelings.

"I can't tell you that. It would ruin the surprise!" Easton

flashed a dimpled grin at me before setting the car in motion.

A wave of excitement washed over me. I didn't let it last long before I protested. Ruining my life's positivity was a bad habit—and one I wouldn't have time to kick.

"I don't know why you're doing this!" I shook my head, angry at the things I couldn't control. Like this feeling like a date, even though it wasn't, and my emotions being all over the place. Why didn't I know what I wanted or how I felt? I pulled my dress down to my exposed knee. I feared he pitied me, even though he made it very clear the night before that he had not.

Easton took a deep breath. "You can't blame a guy for wanting to hang out with a pretty girl, can you?" He tried to diffuse my uprising frustration.

I rolled my eyes. People had told me all my life that I was pretty, but I'd never believed it.

Easton shook my shoulder. "Come on. We're going to have fun tonight. I need some fun," he said.

It was easier for me to think that he needed a distraction, so I went with it, allowing myself to try and believe it. When the image of him standing on the bridge crossed my mind again, I thought it might just be true. We were honest friends, after all.

"So, what do you do for fun normally? You know, when you used to be happy," I asked him and watched as his expression turned dark for a fraction of a second before changing to curiosity.

"Used to be?" Easton's eyes flickered from the road to me.

I looked out the window to the plethora of passing trees. The forest floor blanketed in pine needles and fallen branches. The car wound around the mountainside in tranquility. He didn't want to talk about it; that much was clear. I would have to find another way.

"I mean, your hobbies. Like, I'm in school for graphic design because I love it. I like to take a picture and change it around until it feels balanced and your eye can't help but move across the image in exploration. I've always loved art, ever since I was a kid . . . what's the thing you do, *or did,* that makes you most happy?" I asked, wishing I was comfortable with the silence and didn't feel the need to fill the air with the sound of my voice.

"Well, it isn't so much *what* makes me happy as *who* makes me happy." Easton's eyes flicked back to mine. "And right now, you're making me happy," he said.

Warmth spread across my face, and I lifted my hand to my forehead, subconsciously to cool my blush.

"You're a sweet-talker, Easton Green!" I stifled a laugh, and he did too.

"What!? It's true!" he claimed.

I shook my head, not believing a word he said. "We're *just* friends, and don't you forget it!" I reminded him.

Easton's mouth opened wide in protest, then closed again before saying anything. He scrunched his face, "Well, friends make each other happy, right?"

"Uh, huh." I shook my head as a grin spread across my face.

Our playful banter silenced when we crossed the New

River Bridge. I looked out my window at the dusk lit bridge and decided not to bring up the night we met.

"What do you do for a living?" I asked, surprised that I hadn't thought to do before.

"I'm . . . in construction," Easton said as if he were uncertain how to explain it to me.

I nodded and looked around his car. High-gloss wooden finish and camel colored leather, it still smelled new. It seemed too nice to come from a mountain construction salary. Far too expensive to be driving into a construction zone every day. My eyes lingered on his hands, and though they didn't appear soft, they in no way resembled a man who worked with his hands. I looked from the absent calluses on his hands back to his eyes, where I detected his hesitation.

"I'm in the sales department. I connect the job's manager with the suppliers. It's more social work than anything else," Easton said as he furrowed his eyebrows.

Though it made a lot more sense, something in the back of my head was telling me to be cautious. I rationalized with myself. It explained the scuff-free hands, and he *was* good with people. It made sense for him to be a salesman, and with what I saw at the diner, he could probably make enough extra money in commissions to afford the car.

Though suspicious, I wasn't worried. Easton was more of a puzzle than anything else. I almost preferred the chase. It gave me something to think about other than my illness. The whos and whys of Easton Green dwelled rent-free in my mind. Every omitted truth he told, I stole away to unwrap in thought, late into the night when I was home and alone. It would help keep the terrors away at a bare minimum.

Easton was like my personal mystery novel. I read deep into the night, and I worked tirelessly, trying to find the missing pieces.

I filled the silence by telling Easton the latest about my brother and his engagement. I told him about my parents and how my mom had two sisters that I adored when I was young, but I never saw them now. I told him about how we moved in the fourth grade and how making friends in a new school was easier than I imagined it would be. My mouth didn't stop until we pulled into a packed parking lot forty-five minutes out of Clover. Our headlights illuminated a man and woman walking through the parking lot holding hands. I was relieved to find I wasn't overdressed.

"Where are we?" I asked.

Easton checked his watch and smiled. "Right on time, come on!" He jumped out of his car, ran around to my side, and opened the door for me.

The brisk air rushed in, and a chill ran down my back, causing me to shiver involuntarily. I tucked my clutch under my arm. Easton reached out and rubbed my goosebumps to generate some heat, but his touch caused me to tremble more than before.

"Here." Easton stopped and took off his jacket.

"No! No! You keep it," I crossed my hands back and forth. He threw it over my shoulders anyway. His warmth that lingered inside the jacket now encapsulated me. I smiled at him. "Thank you." I'd seen it happen in the movies, but at twenty-two years old, I had never had a boy offer me his jacket. It made me both happy and sad.

Easton's expression creased with uncertainty when he caught the eye of a man ushering his family through the parking lot. I looked between the two of them.

"Do you know him?" I asked.

Easton guffawed, "Nope!"

The man seemed nice enough. He, too, was dressed in a suit, but unlike Easton, he wore a tie. He wrapped his hand around his little girl's tiny wrist. Easton swallowed hard, keeping his eyes away from the man's. We were all walking in the same direction, into the warmth of the . . . church? My eyes scanned for clues. The stained glass was a big one.

"That's the problem." Easton's gait began to slow. "I don't know him."

The man held the door open for his family and then us. Easton thanked him before taking the load of the door himself. For a moment, I didn't care where we were, as long as I could stay long enough to warm my limbs. But when the wedding march began to play, my heart skipped a beat. I froze. Easton grabbed my hand and pulled me through the double doors right as a bride rounded the corner.

"Easton! No! Wait!" I hissed in protest. He continued to pull me until we were sitting in the last pew—several eyes on us as we made our awkward entrance.

My heart pounded in my chest, and my mouth gaped open. Everyone rose at once. A bride, beaming from head to flawless toe, smiled at us as she walked past on the arm of her father. I threw my hand over my chest to capture my thumping heart and peered over my shoulder at Easton. His expression was that of excitement laced with anxiety.

He leaned in, close to my ear. "Act natural," he whispered, his warm breath tantalizing my ear.

"What!? You don't know these people?" I asked, looking around the room in fear.

I was an imposter. And I felt it too. Surely, we would get caught. We took our seat with the rest of the audience as the ceremony started. My eyes were the size of softballs. Easton held in his laughter, though his body quaked. He raised a fist to his mouth to pretend he was holding in a cough. I smacked him with the back of my hand.

"Are you being serious right now?" I bit my lip and tried not to catch the attention of those around us.

"Shhh. You don't want to get caught!" Easton said.

I seethed. How dare I trust this guy I didn't know! I didn't actually want to crash a wedding! The last thing I wanted was to be put in such an uncomfortable situation. Dew began to form on the back of my neck. I gathered my hair to one shoulder and began to fan myself.

Easton cleared his throat after a small outburst escaped his lips. A little girl with ebony skin and tight black curls turned around in her seat and watched us. If a five-year-old could tell we crashed the wedding, so would everyone else. I shrugged out of Easton's jacket and wiped my clammy palms on my dress, the sweat staining the satin.

As soon as the ceremony was over, I'd be darting to the parking lot.

I shot Easton a look that could kill, but he was too busy crossing off "crash a wedding" on the Hunter's to-go menu across his knee to see it. The realization that he was doing this *for* me and not *to* me dropped like a ton of bricks. He didn't want to be here any more than I did, but here we were because I said I'd never crashed a wedding.

When the groom recited his vows, my anxiety began to melt away. In the presence of love, I no longer had thoughts of fleeing to the car or wanting to kill Easton for bringing me here.

"I promise to cherish you through thick and thin," the groom said.

I listened to his shaky voice and watched as their love was professed in front of their closest friends, family, and the two strangers who snuck into the back pews at the last minute.

"I vow to be your guiding light when the night grows dark and your shoulder to lean on when life is too hard to handle on your own." The groom glanced down at the small piece of paper in his hand.

Easton placed his hand over mine. For reasons unbeknownst to me, I let it linger. His presence reminded me that I wasn't alone. And as much as he needed to have fun tonight, I needed his hand on mine, to tell me it was going to be OK.

When the ceremony ended, Easton pulled his hand back to his lap. The crowd broke out into small social gatherings. Many of the guests retreated straight to their cars. And a small line built in the hall next to the ladies' restroom. I cradled Easton's coat in my arms.

"Thank you for bringing me. I thought you were crazy

at first"—I let out a laugh—"but then I realized this was exactly what I needed."

Easton laughed, "I think I was more nervous than you! But I'm glad we stayed." He smiled down at me. "Think we can survive the reception?"

"What!? No!" I said quickly.

There was no way I was sitting with the bride and groom's aunts and uncles and making up lies about how I knew them.

"I couldn't! Honestly! Don't make me!" I shook my head in all seriousness.

Crashing a wedding sounded fun, but I hadn't considered how nervous I would feel over getting caught. And from the relief in Easton's eyes, I could tell he felt the same way.

Easton chuckled and took the jacket from my arms, proceeding to place it over my shoulders as we walked into the cold with the rest of the crowd. "Are you sure you don't want to? We could stop and get dinner, then sneak back when everyone is toasted. You could even show me your dance moves. What do you say?" Easton asked, wagging his eyebrows.

"Oh, uh-huh, thanks for the offer, but I'm going to have to pass on this one. Plus, we already crossed it off the list." I shrugged apologetically. What was done, was done.

"Oh, thank God!" Easton threw his head back and sighed. "That was giving me indigestion!" Easton laughed at himself with one hand on his stomach. He was cute, trying to be brave for me. I bit the inside of my cheek and tried to cloak my smile. I didn't want to give him the wrong idea.

"Are you hungry? I know of a great place about fifteen minutes from here. It's on the way home too," Easton said as he opened my door.

"A bite to eat never hurt anybody." I tried to sound nonchalant as I crawled into the car. But the truth was, I was taken aback by the selfless gesture he made by taking me to crash a wedding forty-five minutes out of town. And I wanted more of his time.

CHAPTER 10

The dive bar Easton took me to wasn't what I was expecting when he asked me to dinner. We were overdressed, and frankly, I was out of my element. The bar and the wedding alike.

A bum lay outside of the bar. His clothes were tarnished with filth and so was his face. I subconsciously walked to Easton's other side, positioning myself as far away from the man as possible. But it wouldn't be this easy.

"Sam?" The bum struggled to sit up and get a closer look at us. A few beer cans crumpled under his weight, and to my surprise, a small dog appeared, nestled behind him. "Sam? Is that you?" he asked.

I glanced at Easton, hoping he would turn me around and usher me back to the safety of his car, but he did the opposite.

Easton's face softened as he reached for his wallet. He took out all the cash he had and bent down to give it to the deranged man.

"You can do better than this, Simon," Easton said in a quiet voice and handed him the cash. The bum grabbed at the money and started to count. I looked at Easton for an explanation, but he pretended not to notice.

Cigarette smoke marinated in the air, and a lively, probably drunken poker game carried on in the back corner. A pool table sat in the middle of the room where a man in a red plaid shirt and tattoos was trying to get lucky with a girl. By the looks of her attire, he would be successful.

"I know it's not much, but I used to come here to play poker all the time. The people are very nice; you have nothing to be worried about." Easton eyed my clenched hand pulling his jacket closed tight across my chest. I imagined that my face gave even more clues about my uncomfortableness.

Easton slapped the bar, catching the bartender's attention.

"Joey! Hey man, how are you?" Easton shook the bartender's hand.

The man with a long, thick black beard and brut body appeared incredibly happy to see Easton. I peeked around at the crowd; it wasn't what I thought when I pictured Easton's peers. Not that I had been thinking of him that intently.

"Who's the lady?" Joey asked.

"This is Everly. Everly, this is Joey, an old friend." Easton gestured to the bartender.

"Hello." I gave Joey a small wave and polite smile, still clenching the jacket closed.

"Hey, have you seen Clyde much lately?" Easton asked as he leaned over the bar and peered at the back poker game.

"No, man. I haven't seen Clyde for a while. He stopped coming in as much about three months ago." Joey picked up a wet glass and began to wipe it with a bar towel.

"Damn." Easton's forehead lined with worry. "If you see him, will you tell him I stopped in looking for him?"

"Yeah, no problem, man! Can I get you anything while you're here? You guys want a drink?" Joey's face lifted, hoping Easton would stay. Mine did the opposite.

"Um, yeah! That sounds great! I'll take a beer." Easton pointed at me.

I sighed. "Can I see a menu please?" I crawled up on the barstool.

"No menu. I got wine—white or red—beer, and hard alcohol. We also got nachos, peanuts, and . . . that's it!" Joey looked around the bar in case something else had slipped his mind.

I glanced down at the small picked-over bowls of peanuts. I thought about how many men didn't wash their hands after using the restroom had dug into the nuts. I assumed the nachos would be equally disgusting.

"I'll have a glass of red wine, please," I said. Joey smiled and turned around to fetch us our drinks.

"Old friend, huh?" I prompted Easton.

I placed my clutch on the bar but didn't take my hand off of it until I made one last glance around the room. He smiled and looked back at Joey before leaning into me.

"He's had a really tough life. I've spent countless hours

on this side of the bar, walking him through life lessons that he hadn't yet learned. I think he's doing better now," Easton said, in a hushed voice.

Joey placed our drinks on the bar, and Easton straightened his back. I felt bad for Joey. I didn't know the details of his life, but I could easily picture how Easton's ability to connect with people had turned him into a counselor of the night.

"And Clyde?" I asked.

Easton's eyes darted away, and I assumed Clyde was a much longer story than Joey's.

"Clyde's my grandpa." Easton shrugged and took a sip of his beer.

His grandpa? I looked back at the couple, which were now making out against the pool table, and I wondered what kind of man Easton's grandpa was. I had my presumptions.

"Yeah, he . . . he's not that close to the family. Never was. When I found out he played poker here, I started coming to build a relationship with him. I've been coming here every couple of weeks to check in on him, but Joey says he hasn't been showing up." Easton looked down at his feet. No doubt to hide the worry in his eyes.

"Do you think he's sick or something?" I asked with growing concern for his grandfather.

"I don't know. Maybe? I don't have his number or address or anything. Joey says he only pays with cash, so I just give him his space when he goes off the grid for a while. Normally, he would reappear. I think it's more of an intermittent sobriety thing than anything else. I think it ebbs and flows with his depression." Easton peaked up at me, his eyes glassed over and filled with emotion.

I wondered about Easton's disconnected family life. I was positive that this was only the tip of the iceberg. I took a sip of wine, my eyes set on his.

"Did you succeed at building a relationship with your grandpa by playing poker here?"

"I did." Easton's smile reached his eyes. "And I learned a lot about poker too. It's quite fun. My favorite part is trying to read everyone's faces. Some are better than others at hiding their hand, but I can tell most of the time—if not *all* the time—when someone is bluffing." Easton chuckled at a distant memory.

"Hey! That's it! That's the thing you do for fun!" I perked up, excited about my discovery. "I just never took you as a gambler. You never cease to amaze me," I said, feeling the wine work its magic and alter my mood.

"Ha, yeah. Well, sometimes you've got to roll with the punches. I've found myself doing a lot of things that I never thought I would. All for a good reason, though." Easton held up a finger to Joey, who promptly brought me another wine.

"Oh! Thank you. You're not having another with me?" I asked.

"I would like to get you home safe." Easton smiled, every bit the responsible gentleman he was.

My first glass of wine did go down relatively fast, and despite being the only option for red wine, it wasn't half bad. Joey took away my empty glass. I took a long sip, and my eyes fixed on the base of my glass.

"Rolling with the punches . . . Is that what I'm doing now? Rolling with the punches?" I asked, wanting desperately to connect with him on a deeper level.

"Yes. It's what everyone does. You have to deal with it. There aren't many other options, you know?" He cocked his head to the side.

"You had a different option, though, didn't you?" I was too cowardly to look him in the eyes.

He sighed, and a stretch of silence spanned between us. "Excuse me, I need to use the restroom. Will you be OK here?" he asked.

I nodded, never looking at him. I regretted it the moment I said it. I always said the wrong thing, digging too deep too fast. I always pried. It was none of my business what was going through his head the moment I met him. And if I kept asking him, I was sure to lose him as a friend. I couldn't afford it.

I finished my wine and found myself eating out of the nut bowl by the time Easton resurfaced. I watched him on the far side of the room, saying hello to the poker players. Everyone seemed to know and love him. They must have all been fifty years and up, and I wondered why Easton would spend his time with a crowd much older and less fortunate than him.

The girl that was previously making out at the pool table slid her hand across Easton's back as she whispered something into his ear. I stiffened, and my stomach churned. I was frozen as I watched her caress him, and I seriously thought about going over there to break it up. But it was over before it started. Still, it was too long.

Did he like her? Did he know her? Did she not see me sitting over here in this sexy dress on *my date*!? It wasn't *really* a date, but *she* didn't know that!

After Easton paid Joey for the drinks, he made his way back to me.

"Are you ready?" his eyes flickered from mine to the peanut bowl my hand was scraping in. Easton looked back towards Joey, "Hey, can I get some nachos to-go?" I felt my cheeks flush.

"Sorry. I don't think I've had much more than a coffee today," I said as I wiped the salt off my hands.

"Don't be. I can get you something more substantial on the way home, but at least this will get you a little something in your stomach."

Easton turned to pay Joey for the second time, and I turned my daggers to the only other lady in the bar. Easton said goodbye and carried my nachos out to the car for me. I once again clenched his jacket tight as the chilly air collided with my warm body. It felt both cold and reviving at the same time—discomfort with a refreshing silver lining.

I stole a few glances at the bum, who was now asleep on the curb. His dog wandered a few feet away, looking for food.

"Hey, Easton? Why did you call that guy Simon? Do you know him?" I asked as I fastened my seatbelt.

"Who?"

"That guy." I pointed to the homeless man. "The one you gave all your money to," I said, confused. He knew very damn well who.

"Oh, no. I don't know him."

"Then why did you call him, Simon?" I asked.

"Um, it was on his sign. You must have missed it," Easton said as we pulled out of the parking lot and onto the main highway.

I thought back to the sign lying next to the pup; I very clearly remembered what it read: "Money Helps."

Easton didn't talk much on the way home. He said a few things here and there, mostly revolving around making me comfortable. I was quieter this time around. Far too interested in my melted cheese and undoubtedly subdued by the wine. I tried not to make a mess in Easton's prestigious car while I ate and stared out the window into the forest, which was black as the night that surrounded it.

Though I was with Easton—who was the only person that presently understood me—I felt the disconnect between us. I knew the answers lied in his mystery, but he didn't let me in. He didn't trust me as I did him. This realization made me feel alone all over again.

I looked at Easton's profile and let my eyes linger. His hair was becoming more unruly as the night progressed. His shirt was now wrinkled and slightly untucked. I wanted him to notice me. To see me. My nachos slumped down into my lap as my interest in them drifted to Easton.

I wondered what it would be like to kiss his lips. Not that measly kiss he tricked me into giving him at the Red Brick Diner, but a real and passionate kiss. My stomach dropped as Easton caught my gaze, and I looked away, blinking several times. I shook away the random thought and popped another chip into my mouth, rolling the salt between my fingers and trying to keep my mind off of what I really wanted.

"I had fun tonight," Easton offered into the silence.

I smiled. "Me too," I said.

I remembered him holding my hand when the groom recited his wedding vows and how my stomach felt weird and anxious. Maybe it was the cheese, perhaps it was the wine, but if I knew one thing to be true, there was a very strong possibility that it might be because I liked Easton Green. Not in the way I had been telling myself for the last week—the part about us being friends—but in the way that my life was ending, and all I wanted to do was spend my last days with him.

CHAPTER 11

The realization that I had feelings for Easton made the last fifteen minutes of the drive nearly unbearable. I fought through a small panic attack, and to my knowledge, I hid it well enough that it went unnoticed. I tried my damn hardest to push every single thought that came into my head, *out!* I didn't want to know about them, and I told myself that maybe it was just the wine talking. It wasn't, though. I knew that much.

We pulled into my driveway. My palms were sweating and my mind racing. Was he going to kiss me? We stepped out of the car, and he escorted me to my front door, his hand on the small of my back. I trembled as I dug for my key and Yeti serenaded us through the wood door.

"I just wanted to say, that—"

"Thanks! See ya!" I opened my door and slammed it in his face. Shutting the door of opportunity and heartache all the same. Yeti pushed her nose against my thigh as my eyes bulged out of my head, surprised by my own actions. I stood still and listened for Easton's movement, but as far as I could tell, he was just as stunned by my behavior as I was. My heart pounded against my chest. As quietly as I could, I took a step forward and lifted onto my tippy toes to look out my peephole. He was there, rubbing his chin in reflection. There we were, so close and yet worlds apart. But the thickness of the door wasn't the only thing that stood between us.

Two times he turned to knock on the door but ultimately gave up entirely and walked to his car. My heart continued to race. I lowered down, my heels pressing into the floor, and rested my forehead on the door.

This world was cruel. Like a black hole that swallows you slowly, torturing you along the way. I turned and threw my clutch at the wall and screamed at the top of my lungs, thankful that Easton was long gone and unable to hear my cries. The wrecking quakes hurtled through my body as tears washed down my cheeks. My nails dug into the back of my arms when I tried to comfort myself with a hug. Gripping tight like I might just lose myself all together if I didn't hold on for dear life. Only after noticing a feeling that should have been recognized as pain, did I realize I was squeezing too tightly. I didn't stop. The tiny sting from each fingernail was a blessed distraction from the terror that lived in my head.

My knees began to weaken, and my back slid down the door till my butt was resting on the carpet, and the loud, ugly sobs filled my empty home.

I fought it the best I could. The love I felt for him. I

fought it, because It didn't make any sense to have when I knew it was fleeting.

Still, it grew.

I paid it no attention until it was too late; it'd taken hold of me. Like a vice around my chest and a weight around my ankle. And now what was I supposed to do? Add heartbreak to my bucket list? Or heart*breaker*? Assuming he may have feelings for me too.

It didn't matter if he did or didn't. All of it was equally tragic because I was a girl who was dying. And he was a boy who was not.

CHAPTER 12

The following day passed in a blur. It mostly consisted of me lying in bed, somewhere between sleep and consciousness, but I can't be sure. The curtains were drawn to black out the light, and a pillow covered my head for most of the day. At one point in time, Yeti made sure I couldn't ignore her, so I let her outside. It was then, when I was on two feet, that I picked up my clutch and checked my phone. It was shattered. Dead. If Fresh Grounds was calling me, I wouldn't have known.

I didn't let myself think of Easton. It was probably better to say goodbye now. As I did the night before with a slammed door between us. It would be easier this way.

At some point in the night, I woke. Only slightly to ponder if this was it. Was I dying now? *Could* I die now? I watched my favorite movie in my head. Nicholas Sparks' *The Notebook*. The two were so deeply connected to one another, their love carried them away. I willed it to happen to me. But each subsequent breath told me it was impossible. There was no love train out of this misery. And there was no easy way out. I was stuck, riddled with cancer and a broken heart, determined to stay in my bed until the day I was blessed to leave it all behind. Like a sweet release from the dark thoughts that plagued me.

Miraculously, at some point, I began to dream again. The swans from *The Notebook* surrounded me, and I, too, became a bird in flight.

The never-ending weekend finally came to an end. I had school today. And though I didn't care about learning anything new in the field of graphic design, I figured I could at least get out of the house. Sit in my truck with a piece of paper and pen. If I was fortunate enough, I'd manage some freshly combed hair and a full belly too. I was depressed and run down—miserable at best—but I didn't have to spend my last months bedridden.

By the time I got to school—teeth and hair successfully brushed—I was too late to make my first class. I didn't bother bringing my phone, as I never had the energy to plug the thing into the wall to recharge it. Still, it sat dead and shattered in my entryway. The less distraction, the better, I figured. I looked at my notebook, which sat beside me in the passenger's seat. I was going to need caffeine to get through writing these letters.

I was too much of a coward to stop at the coffee shop before school, so I walked to the vending machine for a Diet Coke.

The gentle rumbling of my engine soothed my nerves. I placed my notebook on my lap and the pen in my hand. I didn't know how to start, but I figured "Dear Mom," was as good of a place as any. I wrote nothing but the truth. Easton would be proud. I told her how I was sorry for not telling her of my illness sooner. I told her I was sorry for not letting her in. And I told her that I would change it if I could. If I was brave enough. The letter went on and on—nine pages of regrets and goodbyes. A few short, memorable stories that I held dear to my heart. I was only vaguely aware that the change of class had come and gone with the students around my truck.

I didn't cry. If anything, I felt the baggage I had been carrying lift. College was back in session, so I took out a clean piece of paper and continued to write. "Dear Pop," This letter wasn't as long and sappy. I didn't worry about crushing his soul like I did my mom's. He was a strong and capable man, and he would be the rock that held the family together.

When I got to my brother's letter, I found myself without words. All that I wanted to write was *Don't marry Chloe*, but it wasn't what I wanted him to remember me for. If he married that girl and his life turned out to suck the way I imagined it would, well then, I would be there to sit by his side in misery. It would be hell for both of us, I suppose. I sighed, finished my Coke, and wrote a nice letter, filled with my best memories of us as kids. I only mentioned once that if he ever happened to fall, I would be there to help him pick himself up again.

It was lunch break when I had three complete letters

resting in my notebook. I stepped out of the truck to use the restroom and hit up the vending machine one more time. The wet grass beneath my shoes, the chilly spring air, and the buzzing studentry were invigorating enough to make me want to attend my last class. And that I did.

It would be one of the last times, though. I couldn't concentrate in the least. I found myself looking at the students one by one and wondering what their lives were really like.

Was her skirt so short because she didn't have a loving father? Did she show off her body because it was the only way she knew how to get attention from men? Or did she simply like the way it looked on her?

My eyes floated to a guy who was unquestionably the high school outcast. He most likely played in the band and had never been to third base. His acne would have prevented him from getting close to anyone. I wondered when he would peak. He would be rich in his forties, own a large advertising firm, and do it all with ease. He'd have a clear complexion, too. I wished I could tell him to wait just a little longer—that his time would come.

I looked down at my keyboard and smiled when I seriously considered telling the outcast my premonition. Trying very much to be like Easton at the diner, my intentions would be golden, but it would come out all wrong. I would end up telling him that one day he would no longer be a virgin, and his zit face would clear up. All he would take away from the conversation was that he was a loser, and I'd end up doing more harm than good. My smile faded as I concluded that I didn't have Easton's touch. And some things are better left alone.

When I pulled into my driveway, I was shocked to see my mom's car waiting for me. *Damn.* I was going to hear it from my mom. This and that. Me not answering my phone . . .

"Mom?" I called out to her.

"Everly? Where have you been!? I've been worried sick over you. The least you could do is answer your mother's phone calls!" She shook her head in aggravation and continued. "You don't answer your phone for two days! You weren't at work! Lindsay said you never came in or called out si—"

"Mom! Please, stop."

My eyes rolled into the back of my head. Ugh. Now I have to deal with this too? I noted the clutch on the ground, right where it had landed. My shattered phone on the entry table. Had she seen it?

"Why don't you go to the living room, let me get changed, and I'll make you some tea." I coaxed her away from the phone, and when she was out of sight, I hid it under a school binder.

"You can't do that again. Do you understand me? Just because you live in this house and not under our roof doesn't give you the right not to call me back. I'm your mother! And I always will—"

"Mom! I get it. Please. I won't do it again!" I shrugged. There was nothing else I could say. The next time would surely be the last.

"OK, OK!" My mom held her palms up to show her

compliance. "We're having dinner tomorrow night, and your father and I want you to bring that boy you're seeing. I think you owe us that after this little stunt you pulled." Mom gestured to the space between us.

Just when I was about to swear Easton off altogether, I needed him to appease my parents. Funny how that works. I imagined his face through the peephole, and I cringed. If I wanted him to come to my parents for dinner and pretend to be my boyfriend, I was going to have to explain to him what happened the night I slammed the door in his face. I would rather die.

"Sure, Mom. Tomorrow. I'll see if he's available. There's a chance he'll be busy, but I'll ask anyway."

I took off my jacket and made my mom a black tea. She followed me into the kitchen, telling me the latest news regarding the wedding. I kept my mouth shut when Mom said that Chloe wanted daisies on every table. There was nothing romantic about daisies.

"What is that?" Mom came up behind me and grabbed at my arm.

My stomach dropped as I yanked my arm back to my side. I took a quick peek. It was nasty—all five fingernails. The scabs like crescent moons.

"Is that boy hurting you!?".

"No!" I stood with my mouth open, ready to explain anything that would clear Easton's name, but nothing came. It made him look all the more guilty.

"Oh, honey!" Mom said, her voice about to crack with emotion and her eyes glassing over.

"No, seriously, Mom. It's not—"

My mom collided with me, wrapping her arms around my back and squeezing tight. God, what did I get myself into?

"You're not listening to me!" I pushed away from her embrace. Her eyes were red, her heart breaking for me. And she didn't even know the truth. She couldn't handle the truth. It was a good reminder.

"I did it," I said—shame pouring out of me for losing control and for being too cowardly to admit why.

"You? Why would you do that? No, that's a man's hand! I can tell!" Mom grabbed my hand, now angry that I was covering for my boyfriend.

I wrapped my arms around myself and placed each finger in its hole, aligning the nails with the scabs. Mom stared in revelation. I think it hurt her more to know the person she loved was also the one she needed to protect me from. It would have been easier for her to wrap her head around a guy mishandling me. At least then, she could be angry. Now, she didn't know what to feel.

"It was an accident. I had a . . . panic attack, and it kind of just took over. I was trying to comfort myself with the security of a hug, but I was just too aggressive, I guess. I didn't even know I was doing it. I'm not trying to hurt myself, I promise." I said.

"A panic attack?"

"Yeah, I'm starting to get them. They've been coming on over the last couple of months. All the stress, I guess."

"What stress?" she asked, catching me in my lies.

I had no right to stress. I was twenty-two, worked in a coffee shop, and went to school for the arts.

"Self-inflicted stress?" I asked, unsure if that was even a thing.

"Maybe you should talk to someone? You know Maggie down the street has this counselor she's been—"

"Mom, no, I don't need to see anyone. Um, actually, Easton's been helping me get through it!"

"He is?" she asked.

"Yeah, you know, he talks to me in the middle of the night if I can't sleep. We text all the time. He makes me laugh. He's really good for me." I threw it all at her . . . anything I could to put her worried mind to rest.

Mom nodded and ran her hands down my arms. "OK, then. You just let me know if you need that number," she began.

"I will let you know, but as of right now, I'm just fine."

"OK, dear," Mom said, her voice laced with worry.

"What time tomorrow?" I asked. I had quite the show to put on now.

CHAPTER 13

eck! Where have you been!" Lindsay hissed at me when I walked behind the bar at Fresh Grounds.

"A caramel frappe. Toffee and whipped cream on top," I whispered back.

Lindsay's eyes grew dark. "I was worried," she said.

I sighed, not wanting to deal with her emotions. Mine were already too much to bear. "I'm sorry. I'll call next time."

"Kim, can you take over the register?" Lindsay asked the girl that was busying herself with the espresso beans. She was new and not yet comfortable with the register. Or the lattes. Or common sense. I gave her an encouraging smile as Lindsay pulled me into the back room.

"What the hell has been going on with you? You didn't show up for work, and both your mom and Easton came by looking for you. You didn't ca—"

"Easton came by?" I asked.

Lindsay frowned at my selective hearing.

After a long sigh, the hand on her hip fell to her side, and she said, "Yes. He came by yesterday. He said you weren't answering your phone . . . are you OK?"

"Yeah," I looked to my feet. My stomach sank, as I knew my acting skills were subpar.

"Beck?" Lindsay prompted.

I looked into her eyes. My throat burned as the weight on my chest threatened to crush me.

"I don't want to talk about it."

Lindsay's shoulders dropped. She thought about it for a moment before allowing me my privacy. She was a good friend. The best.

"You know Jacob isn't too happy with you, either. I lied and told him that you called in sick, but I wasn't on the schedule that day, so my story kind of fell to shit. You should pick up some extra hours or something to get back in his good graces."

"I'm not worried about Jacob," I said.

Jacob was my manager. It always bothered me that he was our age and carried no more managing skills than Lindsay or me. I was convinced that he had gotten the position because he was the only man that applied to work at the coffee shop when it opened. If he had a problem with me not coming into work, he could fire my ass.

"I'll make your drink," Lindsay said.

I took my schedule from Jacob's desk and frowned when I saw that I was supposed to work the night shift tomorrow. It would take a little effort on my part, but I was pretty sure Kim would fold and cover my shift.

"Hey, Kim? Can you cover for me tomorrow night? I have dinner plans." I called to her while she busied herself with unnecessary cleaning.

"Sorry! I've got plans." Kim's squinty eyes tried to look apologetic. I wasn't expecting Kim to be anything but meek. As disappointed as I was, I was also a tad impressed that she turned me down.

I sighed and spun around to find Lindsay with my drink in hand.

"I'll cover you," she said and handed me my drink. Whipped cream exploded out of the top, and toffee pressed against the clear lid.

"Oh my God, thank you! Have I ever mentioned how much I love you?"

We both chuckled, but I think that deep down, she knew it was true. We had been friends since we were kids, and while other friends came and went, she was my one constant.

"Oh! I almost forgot! I have your sister's dress in my truck!"

I retrieved the dress. The sun was warm on my shoulders, and the caffeine had lifted my spirits already. My eyes wandered the street, searching for Easton, hoping he would come around today as well. He was nowhere in sight, though.

After patching up my misstep with Lindsay, I went home knowing that my phone should now be fully charged. I had to call Easton, but I feared he would not be so forgiving.

I waited until evening to call. Pacing around my house,

holding my shattered phone in my hands. I was too much of a chicken to listen to the message he had left me. I'm sure it said something about how I ended our date, and I didn't want to relive the embarrassment. I knew I was an idiot. If it were up to me, I would end my relationship with Easton now. Pretend I didn't have fun at the wedding and that my feelings for him were nonexistent. But it wasn't up to me. Not if I had my mom to appease. No, I needed Easton for my charade. How did my life get so complicated right when it was supposed to wind down?

The phone rang in my hands. Easton Green. I stiffened but answered. "Hello?"

"Everly?" Easton asked.

"Yeah, hi." I started to pace again, making small circles around my living room.

"I haven't heard from you. Are you OK?" he asked. The worry in his voice reduced me to guilt.

"Yeah!" I said. My voice high and fake.

Easton waited for the truth. He somehow knew me better than most, and yet not at all.

"Um, I just had a momentary lapse of self-pity. If that's what you would call it." I stopped my fidgeting around the room and leaned against a window. A bird scratched through the dirt, looking for food.

"Yeah. That's a pity party, alright." Easton said in a voice no different than if he were confirming the name of a rare insect. I smiled at his understanding.

"Why wasn't I invited?" he asked.

My smile grew, and the worry slipped away. "I didn't know that was your kind of party?"

"I'm so down to party! I would have brought the sorrow strobe light . . ." I laughed out loud as he continued. "The pity piata . . . the blue balloons—"

"OK! OK! Next time, you're invited!"

"That's what I wanted to hear." Easton paused for a moment. "Everly?" he asked.

"Beck . . . Call me, Beck." My heart melted. I hadn't planned on letting anyone else in. But there he was, making his way into my heart—one word at a time.

"Beck, I mean it. We can put on sad movies, and you can cry on my shoulder and pretend it's about the movie. I'll bring ice cream or just lie next to you when you want to shut out the world. Just don't shut me out too, OK?"

I took a seat on my sofa and mused over his offer. It was an inviting thought. I didn't want to do it alone.

"OK. But only because your pity parties sound so much better than mine." I laughed off the heaviness of the conversation.

"They are. I can guarantee it!"

"Oh, hey Easton. I have to ask a favor of you." I jumped up and began to pace again. This was the worst part.

"Yeah?"

"My parents want to meet my *boyfriend* . . . tomorrow." I cringed, saying the word *boyfriend*. My eyes shut tight, awaiting his response.

"Oh, wait. Is that me?" Easton said.

"Yes! Please?" Biting my lip couldn't help his answer come any faster, but I still tried.

"OK, I suppose I could make you kiss me—just one

more time, though." Easton let out an exasperated sarcastic sigh.

I laughed out loud and was grateful he couldn't see the warmth in my cheeks.

"What! That's not part of the deal, buddy." I played hard to get while my heart fluttered with anticipation for the promise of a kiss.

I didn't have to wait for dinner the next night; it came quicker than a blink of an eye. I wore a plushy pink lipstick and tucked away my nerves. I filled Easton in on who he would meet on the short ride over to my parents' house.

"My dad is super easy to get along with; as long as you show him attention, he'll love you. My brother will probably be more difficult to get to know. His name is Carter, and he will have his fiancée, Chloe, with him. Don't mind her; she's . . . well, you'll see. And you know my mom, so—"

"Don't worry about it. I've got this. You know I went to The Acting Academy of Thomas Kelter?"

"You did!?" I asked, shocked.

"No," he said.

I slapped his shoulder with the back of my hand.

"But you believed me, didn't you?" Easton's expression lightened up, and his dimples drew deep.

I wanted to reach out and touch him again. This time, by the handful. I was in an impossible position. I was falling for this guy. But he didn't know it, and I had to keep it that way. On the contrary, my family had to believe the exact opposite.

"Oh no! All this time I was worried about you, but you're a natural! I didn't even consider me! I can't act! I'm the worst! Everyone sees through my lies! Besides, you and I barely know each other!" My eyes bulged, and I fanned my face.

"Beck, don't even worry. Just act natural. We're friends, right?"

I nodded.

"You like me, right?"

I nodded but a bit slower this time.

"Just act like you're hanging out with your friend. Which you are."

I continued to bob my head as Easton pulled into my parents' driveway. Carter was already here. Easton was right. No acting was required of me. My admiration for Easton was clear to see, and my parents wouldn't need to look further.

We began to walk to the front door, Easton grabbed my hand effortlessly, and through the ease of it all, I forgot it was an act.

He leaned down and whispered in my ear. "But this time, when I kiss you, try not to look so surprised."

Words of wisdom laced with promise. My eyes grew as my mom opened the door before us.

"Honey!" Mom reached her arms out for a grand hug, holding on much longer than usual.

"Hi, Mom. You remember Easton." I gestured to the calm and collected man beside me.

Not a hint of nervousness resided in his face. I marveled at him while my mom embraced him tightly and whispered, "Thank you for taking care of my baby," in his ear. I tried to ignore it, and Easton did a good job of pretending he knew what she was talking about.

"Always," he simply said. And I knew that wasn't part of the act. Mom felt it too.

The smell of spaghetti collided with boisterous introductions. Pop took to Easton immediately, as I had imagined he would. Carter shook Easton's hand with a sideways glare.

I hugged Chloe hello and found myself pleased that her lipstick and outfit were more subdued tonight. But even though her lips were mauve, her energy was still fire hydrant red. She wasn't the one for my brother, and I prayed he would see it before he walked down the aisle.

"Hey, there's my girl!" Before turning back to Easton, my dad squeezed me tightly. "Do you like hockey?" he asked.

It was my cue to leave the men to their sports and grab a glass of wine. I smiled at Easton as he accepted a beer from my dad, and his expression reassured me that he was more than equipped to handle himself alone.

I got a glass of wine and joined my mom in the kitchen. "It smells great, Mom. Thanks for having us," I said.

"Oh, I'm so glad you brought Easton! Your dad has wanted to meet him. Just look at them! They're hitting it off, don't you think?" she asked.

Chloe and I turned to follow my mom's gaze. Easton had the floor. He was telling some elaborate story, his arms reached out wide, and my dad laughed. Carter stood an extra couple feet away, and he chuckled, but it didn't reach his eyes. My brother glanced over at me, and I tried to give him a look that asked he at least try to get to know Easton. I could see him roll his eyes from across the room, but then he took one step closer.

"Oh, he is a cutie! I love that . . . thing he's got going on." Chloe waved her hand above her head.

"Yeah, he's got this hair that—actually it just works—whether it's been styled, or not. It even looks good when it's soaking wet." My eyes unfocused into a distant memory.

"Soaking wet! Ooh, that sounds like a story to me!" Chloe lifted her shoulders to her ears and brought her hands together in prayer. Her fingers tapping ever so slightly into the world's smallest clap. It took everything I had not to express my true thoughts. She wasn't evil; I knew that. It's not like I wished ill will on the girl; I just wished she would find a better match for herself. Someone more . . . I don't know. Shallow.

"There's no story. He's just a really nice guy, that's all." I tried to squash the curiosity burning in Chloe's eyes.

"He *is* a nice guy," Mom said. "He's been there to help Beck with her anxiety."

Mom threw salt into the boiling water. She never thought about keeping her mouth shut. I was used to it by now. She wore her heart on her sleeve and her mind in her mouth.

"Ohhh," Chloe cooed and her doe eyes widened. I could see the emptiness that resided within. Did she *know* what anxiety meant?

"What can I help you with, Mom?" I asked, eager to move the conversation along.

Carter came up behind Chloe and wrapped his arm around her waist. He stole a kiss on her neck, and I looked away.

Mom brushed my offer aside. "Nothing, dear. I've got it all done, anyway."

"So, you really like that guy?" Carter asked, not bothering to hide his feelings the way I did with his fiancée.

I glanced over to Easton; my dad had him fully engaged in the hockey game as he pointed to the screen.

"Yeah, I *really* like that guy," I said as natural as it came. The conversation moved onto the wedding, but my eyes continued to rest on Easton. I couldn't quite grasp how he managed to look so relaxed. As if he were home amongst his own family.

CHAPTER 14

I don't know if it were the warmth of the crackling fire or my apprehension about the topic at the dinner table, but I was sweating bullets. My dad asked Easton how we met, and I was very aware that the truth wasn't a story that could be told. Easton and I shared a quick glance before he chose to rescue me from my atrocious acting skills.

"We met on the New River Bridge," Easton began.

The heat poured over me, and even though I had been keeping my jacket on to hide the self-inflicted pain I displayed on the back of my arms, I could no longer survive being trapped inside the furnace. I shrugged off my jacket and pulled my hair into a ponytail.

"The New River Bridge! Is that right?" My dad engaged.

"Yes, sir. I was driving home from work when I saw Beck standing on the side of the road. She was looking at her flat tire like it was a UFO."

Dad laughed and slapped the table. Even Carter chuckled.

"Ain't that right!" Dad held his beer up towards me. I raised my glass of wine as I rolled my eyes. Easton was so good at this, I couldn't help but wonder why.

"Now, I was in no position to pass a pretty lady in distress. So, I pulled over. After fixing her tire, I asked her out on a date. To this day, I'm not sure if she wanted to or if she did it as a favor, but I like to think I won her over that night." Easton locked eyes with mine and slid his hand onto my knee. "The rest is history," he said.

I barely noticed how happy my mom was. I was too busy basking in the freefall. I don't know how he did it; every word out of his mouth was something to remember and reflect on. He had so much heart, I wondered how he could contain it. I reached down to his hand and squeezed it. We were acting like a couple, true, but we both knew nobody could see our interlocking hands under the table. That one was for us.

When everyone had their fill of dinner, I shrugged my jacket back on so that nobody would see. I helped my mom clean the dishes, and Easton attempted to win over my brother. It was no easy task, but I applauded him for trying. Mom scraped the leftover meatballs into a container, and Chloe collected placemats as she rambled on about the recipe she followed for the chocolate mousse pie she brought. As unsettled as the nerves had made my stomach, I was pretty sure there was a separate compartment made of steel that only always accepted dessert.

When the kitchen had been put back together, I rescued

Easton from my brother. If he was as relieved as I imagined he should be, he didn't show it. He followed me to my parent's back patio. Small and quaint. A rose garden with a fountain and a view of the night's starry sky. I took a deep breath of the refreshing cold air and walked to the back fence line. The furthest away from the house, with the most privacy.

"How are you holding up?" I asked Easton.

"Don't worry about me. I'm solid. How are you?"

"I'm good. I can't thank you enough for coming tonight. You've made my mom very happy." Easton wrapped his arm around my shoulders, and though the cool air felt nice, I huddled close to him.

"I'm glad she's happy. You have an amazing family. You should consider yourself lucky," Easton said.

"Lucky?" I asked.

"Well, you know what I mean." He shrugged.

"Yeah, I do." I looked up into the stars, and after a stretch of silence, I said, "I *am* lucky."

Of course, I only saw that when I was with him.

Easton took advantage of my extended neck and lowered down to my lips. I didn't fight it. I couldn't. I lifted to my toes and closed the distance. He wrapped one arm around my waist and slid the other to my cheek. I kissed him long and deep, my passion and fear both exploding into fireworks. In that moment, I felt more alive than ever before. And by the time my heels returned to the floor, I knew I was falling in love.

"Um," I said, "you're quite the actor."

Easton shook his head. "You *know*."

It was all he had to say. I nodded and buried my head into his chest. "I know," I said.

We remained tight in the embrace for some time until Chloe yelled, "Time for dessert!"

I smiled. "I don't want to leave. And I *love* dessert. What are you doing to me?" I asked.

I looked up to see his expression. It seemed that I wasn't the only one fighting my feelings, and worry creased in my forehead.

"Is something wrong?" I asked, knowing damn well that my whole world was burning down.

Easton shook his head and smiled down at me. While I couldn't detect a difference in his smile, I could feel it in my heart. Something was wrong. I felt it like a bird with clipped wings. Our love had a ceiling.

"Let's get some of that pie before it's gone." Easton patted my back, and we made our way inside.

The dessert would have tasted better if I wasn't swallowing my emotions. One bite at a time. It did nothing to help.

As the night came to an end, we said our goodbyes and left hand in hand. And when the door closed behind us, I was unsure whether to let go or not.

Easton drove me home, neither one of us speaking. I stared out the window at the passing headlights and allowed myself to be swallowed by my fear. Only this time, it wasn't the cancer. This time, it was losing Easton.

When Easton pulled up to my house, neither one of us got out of the car. He set the car in park, and faint barks from Yeti sounded from the house.

I unbuckled.

"You have to tell them," Easton said.

"Tell them what? That we're not together?" I asked.

"No, never mind that. You have to tell them about your condition."

"Why!"

"Because!" He ran his hand through his hair in distress. "You'll regret it if you don't!"

"Huh, no . . . actually, I'll be dead, and the last time I checked, dead people don't muse over their past mistakes. And if there is such a thing as heaven, do you really think they'll allow regret through those pearly gates?!" The roller coaster continued.

Easton fumed. Quick breaths expelled from his nostrils like a fire breathing dragon. We were feeding off each other as the frustration of an impossible situation grew larger. But the truth was, he didn't know any better than I did about what happens after we die. He had no right telling me how I would feel. And judgment was the last thing I needed on a very long list of unmet needs. My heart pounded, and the tears burned my eyes. I should have waited for him to answer, but I continued to tear into him instead.

"You know, Easton, whatever we've got going between us, maybe it's better if it just ends now," I said. I got out of the car and slammed my door.

Easton jumped out after me but came to a stop at his taillights.

"End? Beck, come on." Easton's voice softened.

"No! Seriously. What the *fuck* is the point in all this? In you and me? We get close, and then it just makes everything that much harder? Why are we doing this to ourselves? It's a slow burn of torture, and while I might not live with the *regret*, you will! Is that what you want?" My tone sharp and forthcoming.

Easton took a step towards me. I took a step back.

"Beck. Don't do this," he said, holding out a hand.

My eyes dropped to the extended invitation to spend my last days in his arms. The cost? Shattering his heart in the wake of my departure.

"It's what I want," I said, sure of myself.

Our eyes lingered on each other for what seemed to be an eternity of pain and suffering. It was my hell on earth. Giving up the only man I'd ever loved. Setting him free in hopes that it would be in his best interest. I would have no way of knowing.

Easton closed the distance between us and brought his lips to my forehead. A warm soft kiss planted on my soul. And then he was gone. I didn't watch him leave.

I was mistaken when I thought it couldn't get any worse than the night that I scarred my arms. I crawled into bed, still half-dressed, and closed my eyes for the sweet escape of slumber. As it turns out, not feeling anything at all was worse than any pain I'd ever encountered. The roller coaster had stopped, and the numbness carried me away into a deep and loveless sleep.

CHAPTER 15

The numbness followed me like a shadow; only, it was there regardless of the light. I went to work and school but only to keep my mind off Easton.

When Dawson finally approached me in class, I was relieved to think about someone other than Easton. I couldn't believe that Dawson was my typical type. I used to drool over his abs—any abs really. Now I found myself attracted to Easton's body. The thick muscles of Dawson made me wonder if he would sink in a body of water, and I wondered where the days had gone when he danced around my head shirtless. There were no more dreams of soap suds and dripping sponges.

Easton ruined it all for me. I would never look at another male specimen the same. I only wanted Easton and his beautiful soul.

I skipped a few of my classes to sit in my truck and write one more goodbye letter. This time it was to Easton. Everything poured out with ease—all of my thoughts but none of the emotion. And I had a lot of thoughts. It all made sense to me. Easton was better off without me. My mind told me so. I detailed it in my letter. It was a simple note, only a one-pager. In the last paragraph, I professed that I loved him and that my only regret was not telling him in person. I signed the letter with a heart and prayed to God that heaven didn't allow regrets.

It'd been six days since I broke it off with Easton, and he called only once. I cleared his call when he did, and he never left a message. I would be lying if I said I never thought about calling him back. I did . . . all the time. But it was my love for him that kept me away. And it was my numbness that allowed me to survive the heartache.

On the seventh day, I decided to take a drive and wound up sitting in the parking lot of the dive bar Easton had taken me to. The bum was gone, and so was his dog, but the trash he left behind still remained. I parked and watched as a trickle of customers walked inside and never came out. It was only 3:30 p.m., but I assumed that addiction knew no time. Somehow, being here at the bar made me feel a little closer to Easton, and I wanted to savor it. My next stop would be the bridge, and I imagined that I would feel his presence even stronger there.

When I decided to continue on with my pathetic road trip, an older gentleman walked out of the bar on his cell phone. I cracked my window to listen to his conversation. Because I was a small-town girl from Clover, and that's what we do best.

"What? I can't hear you! Wait . . . that's better! Go on,"

the man said. He was slender—all but his belly, and I was pretty sure that he might be pregnant.

"No! No! Bring it by the bar. I'll be here 'til closing," he said.

Watching a drug deal wasn't going to bring me any closer to Easton, so I started my ignition.

It was through the rumble of my old truck that I heard him say, "Don't you Clyde me, you chicken shit!"

Clyde?

I stepped on my brake. My eyes shot around, suddenly aware of my surroundings. Clyde was Easton's grandfather! My heart picked up speed. What was I to do?

Clyde hung up the phone and grumbled a string of profanities. I feared he would walk into the bar and be lost forever.

I pulled out wide and stopped next to Clyde as he lit a cigarette. My window dropped slowly, causing him to step off the curb and approach my car.

I panicked.

"Do you know how to get to Clover from here?" My forehead drenched with worry.

"Oh, yeah." Clyde rested his forearm on my window seal and waved about his cigarette with the other hand. "Go south on Falcon—"

"Are you Clyde?" I blurted out.

The man looked at me with trepidation.

"Who's askin'?"

"Um, I'm a friend of Easton Green's, and—"

"Ohhh! Well, why didn't you say so!? How's that fella doin'?" he asked with a bright face.

"Good, yeah, he's good. Um, he misses you. He brought me here a little over a week ago looking for you," I said.

"Is that right!?" Clyde looked a little confused.

"Yeah, he said he hadn't seen you in a while and was worried."

"Oh, yeah. Well, I'm back now. Tell him to come by so I can whoop his ass in poker, would ya?" Clyde chuckled.

I knew I would no longer be talking to Easton to pass on the message.

"Yeah, I can do that. Um, maybe you should call him or something to let him know you're doing OK?" I interjected myself in a place I knew I had no business being. But I felt terrible for Easton. All he wanted was a relationship with his grandpa, and he had to gamble to get it.

"Call him? Well, shit!" Clyde took a long drag off of his cigarette and blew the smoke just outside my window. "I don't have that kid's number or nothin'," he said.

I frowned. "You don't have your grandson's phone number?" I asked him and immediately regretted my judgment.

"Grandson!?" Clyde scowled. An uncomfortable moment passed as my mind raced to fix what I had done.

"Is that kid in some kind of trouble?" Clyde asked. His face creased with the deep grooves of age.

"No! No, sorry, I think I was mistaken. Have a nice day." I placed my truck in drive, and Clyde took a step back, perplexed.

I pulled away quicker than I wanted to, and my tires made a small screeching noise that made me look even more suspect.

What the heck was that!? Easton lied to me? About his family, nonetheless. I traced back through my memory. There was no mention of his family at all except for what he told me about his grandpa. Why was he hiding from me? He was so comfortable on my sofa in the presence of my dad that it made it hard to believe he wasn't brought up in a loving home himself. I couldn't think of another reason for lying, though—other than being ashamed about where he came from.

I replayed every conversation we ever had. Most of it was about me, my life, and my predicament. Never once did he tell me what he was afraid of. He never added to the bucket list. His job was broad and somewhat unfitting. I didn't know what he liked to do, other than poker, and even that was soiled now. I didn't know Easton Green at all. And yet I loved him all the same.

I parked my truck on the side of the road by the New River Bridge. I got out and walked to the very spot his feet had stood on the railing, and I rested my forearms there. The river below was fuller now due to the major storm we had that night. It was the angel's tears that filled up the stream. I thought they were crying for me and my ill-willed fate. But as I looked out into the vast forest where the water met the sky, I realized something. They were crying for him.

Tears leaked from the corners of my eyes. My body was quiet, too damaged to feel the pain. I must have stood there for an hour. Maybe two. Not contemplating the end of my life but consumed with the mystery of his.

I didn't know much about him, but I knew his soul. It left its prints all over mine. Even though I put up a good fight, I knew we were meant to find each other. Like magnets, our destiny intended to collide. What I couldn't grasp was why. What lesson was I supposed to learn from falling for someone I couldn't have? And just like that, I realized it.

It wasn't about me, it never was. He needed me, probably more than I needed him. My life was next to over, but his wasn't. I didn't know my part yet, but I was sure I was meant to help move him along in some way or another.

I checked my watch. My shift at Fresh Grounds started in thirty minutes. I didn't want to leave Lindsay hanging, and since Jacob was working our shift, I thought I better show my face.

I was pleased when I walked into the shop, and the place was empty. Both Jacob and Lindsay sat chatting instead of working. Sometimes the night shifts were the best. Others, we would be bombarded with book clubs and first dates.

"Hey guys," I said, slipping my apron over my head.

"Hey!" Lindsay replied with large strained eyes.

She had something to tell me, but clearly, it would have to wait. Jacob nodded his head towards me and continued with his story about a feud with his cable company. *Good luck with that.* I ducked into the back room and took my time clocking in. I hated nothing more than terrible customer service, and even listening to someone else's story about it would make my anxiety start to rise.

I peeked around the corner to see if they were done—they weren't—but a third person caught my eye on the recliner in the corner. I watched intently as it became clear to me that it was Easton. His eyes were sunken and framed with dark circles. He looked unsettled, and I wanted to take it all away. Whatever it was.

I stepped out from the back room and watched as Easton caught my line of sight. Lindsay pointed in Easton's direction and grabbed my arm, pulling me close.

"He's been here since my shift started, over two hours ago," Lindsay whispered. Then, she gave Jacob an exasperated look to continue with his dreadful story. At least she was getting paid to listen to it.

I walked out to Easton. He stood, his eyes bluer than I'd ever seen.

"You found me . . ." I said.

Easton nodded, "I found you," he mirrored. His face was long, and I could see the pain he had tucked inside.

"Look"—he glanced over at Lindsay and Jacob to make sure we had our privacy—"I know you made your decision, but I can't help but be drawn to you. I can't move on from this," he said.

My body slumped. All of the numbness beginning to wear on me.

"I can, because I know it was in your best interest," I said.

"It's not!"

I smiled. "How do we know we're making the right decision?" I asked.

"I know." Easton placed his hand over his heart. "With the knowledge of three hundred years, I know."

The numbness shattered like glass, falling to the ground. I was in. Whatever it meant, wherever it went, I was in. I slammed into his chest, wrapping my arms around him tightly.

Easton pulled me back to look at my face. "Hey, want to get out of here?" he asked.

I looked between him and my manager. Jacob took his apron off; he must have been planning on leaving early due to the slow night.

"Yes!" I said to Easton.

I looked to Jacob, as he secured his baseball hat on his head and walked out from behind the bar.

"Jacob, I'm taking the night off!" I called out to him. He froze. Lindsay's eyes darted back and forth between the two of us.

"You can't. I'm leaving, and Lindsay can't close the place by herself," he said.

My eyes shot to Lindsay just as she gave me an approving nod of her head. My heart pounded with excitement.

"Then . . . I quit!" I said, wishing it came out more boss than it did. Easton sucked in a breath, and Lindsay's jaw dropped.

I took off my apron and placed it on the bar, giving Lindsay a wink.

"You can't," Jacob started.

"I just did!" I called on my way out.

"Call me!" Lindsay yelled as the door swung closed.

As soon as Easton and I were in the open air of freedom, we began to laugh. I'd never seen him laugh like this; it was beautiful and enormously contagious. We laughed so hard we cried, and I was forced to cross my legs so that I remained a lady. I didn't know where we were going, but we couldn't stay, so we crawled into Easton's car and took off. The laughter faded, and like aftershocks of an earthquake, it would come back now and then.

"Ohhh my God! That was . . . one of the best moments of my life! I feel so . . . free?" I looked to Easton for validation.

He nodded his head. "Free!" he confirmed.

"How should we celebrate my retirement?" I chuckled.

"I know a place." A coy expression spread across Easton's face.

"Come on, no secrets this time. Where are we going?"

"We have another bucket list item to cross off. The truck is packed, just in case I was lucky enough to win you over," Easton grabbed my hand in his and brought it to his lips. He kissed it. "We're sleeping under the stars."

"We're going camping?"

"Yup. I have sleeping bags, a tent. Marshmallows . . . And now you."

CHAPTER 16

I worried for the vanity of Easton's BMW as he rolled over thick tree roots and rocks, only wincing when I'd hear the bushes scrape the length of the car. If he cared, he didn't show it. It was dark out when we reached the clearing. He seemed to know the place by heart and took no wrong turns.

"How prepared are you, exactly?" My eyes tried to stretch the distance but couldn't see past the glare of the window.

"I know what I'm doing!"

"But it's going to be cold, and there are probably bears, right?" I asked in a tone of worry as my excitement melted into apprehension.

"Oh my God, Beck! I told you, you wouldn't like it, but you wanted to sleep under the stars! You romanticized this in your head, and I've vowed to give it to you!" Easton reached over and jabbed a few fingers into my ribs, causing me to giggle. "Now get your butt out of the car, bears and all, because we have work to do."

I opened my door and stepped onto the gravel, afraid of what I couldn't see. Easton and I met at his trunk, where he pulled a beanie over my head. He had thought of everything.

"Grab the tent and place it in the clearing. You can get to work unrolling it. I'm going to try to get a fire started," Easton said.

I grabbed the tent and walked out to the beams of the headlights. I unrolled the tent and pulled the corners as far as I could to make a square. Several sticks cracked under my feet, startling me each and every time. I never thought I would die in the woods at the hands of a bear, but the reality was slowly sinking in. Even though I was frightened of the vast wilderness at night, I couldn't think of a place I would rather be than here with Easton underneath the Milky Way.

A small sense of pride lingered after I completed my first task. I took it one step further and turned the poles into two long straight sticks. Easton had been successful with the fire, and flames jumped, hungry for more dried leaves and deadwood. With his help, the tent went up easy, and I was eager to get the bedding inside and zip up the door, closing out all of the nocturnal eyes.

Once the tent's inside was complete, Easton took four large rocks and placed them by the fire. He pulled bottled waters out of his truck and emptied them into an old beat-up canister that he placed on top of the fire. I smiled at the amount of effort he had put into tonight.

"What if I had said no?" I asked.

"Said no to what?"

"Tonight. Would you still have gone camping?" I huddled in the door of the tent.

Easton laughed. "Do you really think I would torture myself for no good reason?"

"Hey!" I laughed. "It's not that bad, is it?"

Easton plopped down next to me, resting his forearms on his knees. "Nothing is *that* bad when I'm with you," he said.

"But a little bad? You can admit it!" I poked his side.

He wrestled my hand. "Yeah, you're a total pain in my ass. It's bad! It's bad, alright!" he pulled on my hand, drawing me in and kissed me. "I've got it . . . *bad* . . ." My heart sang, my head swam, and my body propelled towards Easton. He barely caught me, and our bodies hit the floor of the tent with force. I struggled to kiss him and rip my jacket off at the same time. He rolled me over, and the weight of his body compressed mine. His woodsy cologne intoxicated me with a desire I'd never felt so sure of. I pulled him in close with the free hand I had, running my hand up into his hair. I tightened my grip on its silky texture—my other hand pinned inside the arm of my jacket. I moaned, lifting my hips into his.

Easton pulled back, both of us out of breath. He stared at me for a moment before whispering sweet warmth into my ear. "We have all night."

His words did nothing to break the urgency I felt. I needed him *now*. "Isn't this what you want?" I lifted my head and planted slow seductive wet kisses down his neck.

"Beck," he said, his voice laced with pain. I pulled away to see his eyes. "You have no idea!" he shook his head.

I was more than surprised when he rolled off of me. He brought both hands up to his head and grabbed hold.

I perched up onto an elbow, "Wha—"

Easton ran his palms down his face and covered his eyes.

"What is it then? I mean, don't stop on my account. I want to do it! I do!" I begged him to hear my words. I leaned in to kiss him again. This time, he shied away.

"I know, I know. I just, I don't want to take advantage of you," he said.

My old friend, anger, began to rumble in my blood. I struggled to keep my voice calm. "Are you telling me . . . that this is a cancer thing? Now?"

Easton pulled his hands away and gave me the full weight of his heavy heart through his eyes.

"This has nothing to do with that and everything to do with me."

"What, it's not you, it's me? That's the line you're trying to feed me right now?" I accused him.

"No! That's not it at all!" Easton studied my face. He couldn't possibly understand my anger.

"The truth is that I care for you." Easton shook his head, and the gloss in his eyes sparkled by the light of the fire. "More than you'll ever know. It's like I've waited my *whole* life for you. Now, I don't want you to feel rejected . . ."

I rolled my eyes and looked away. He totally understood, apparently more so than I did, but I was embarrassed that it was as simple as that. Rejection.

"But Beck, I can't move this relationship any further than where it is. You don't *know* me . . . and if you did, I don't think you'd feel the same way."

I furrowed my eyebrows. What was he talking about? I didn't need to know where the guy grew up to know I loved him.

"I can't do that to you. I can't have you fall for a guy you can't know. And, I know how you feel. I see it when you look at me. I feel it too," he said.

I watched the flames flicker in his eyes, as he watched our water boil and spit out of the canister. Neither one of us cared to remove it from the fire.

My anger fell to the wayside, and I placed my hand on his back, the moment of lust and fury now behind me.

"Tell me?" I asked. I was ready for it. Whatever skeletons he had in his closet, I was ready to meet them face to face.

"I can't." Easton shrugged.

"Yes, you can. And I won't go anywhere."

He continued to shake his head, his eyes fixated on the boiling water.

"Easton?" I asked, and when he refused to look at me, I wrapped my hand around his chin and pulled his face to meet mine. I placed a soft kiss on his lips and whispered, "I'm falling in love with you. And there's nothing that you can say that will turn me away. I'm in this for the long run." I scuffed. "Or *my* run, however long that may be."

Easton pressed his forehead to mine and my heart ballooned out of my chest.

"I've been falling since the day I met you on the bridge.

I've never hit the ground so hard, and I'm afraid of what it will do to me when you're no longer here," Easton confessed. I nodded. It was what I was worried about for him.

"There are only two options. We do it wholeheartedly, or we don't," I said. But there was a third choice that I left out on purpose. The one where we stay together without ever scratching his surface.

"I've made my decision. That's why I'm here tonight. Risking my life with paper thin shelter, and a real chance of being frozen alive," Easton joked.

"I'm here too. I know it's the right decision for me, and I really hope that somehow it's the right decision for you too," I said.

"It is. You don't worry about me. OK?"

"OK," I said.

"Promise?" he asked.

"Promise." This thing was going to be hard for both of us. But somehow, we couldn't escape it. We were bound together by a weird and mystical force, unseen by the human eye.

"At some point, Easton, you're going to need to open up to me."

It took some time for an answer, but finally, he said it. "I know."

I rested my head on Easton's shoulder till my heart began to slow, and the tension lifted away. My eyes grew heavy, and the fire died down to ash and embers. I crawled into my sleeping bag and Easton placed the heated rocks from the fire near our feet. I snuggled up to him, lying my head on his arm as we watched the stars twinkle from the top of our tent. We saw three shooting stars that night. And all of my wishes were for Easton's walls to drop.

I didn't try to kiss him again. There was a kind of honor between us. He didn't want to feel like he was tricking me into loving him, but he also wasn't ready to talk. I had no other choice but to wait. Ironically, time was the only thing I couldn't give to Easton.

I was no princess, but I sure did feel all the peas lying on the forest floor that night. Worse yet, I heard all of the sounds of the living. And at one point in the night, I sat up and armed myself with a flashlight.

I woke at first light. The bags under my eyes were probably a close match to Easton's, but I was happy. Waking next to him was a gift, and I felt blessed to cross another item off my bucket list.

"Coffee?" Easton asked as he lit a new fire.

"Please." My voice cracked, and I coughed the morning phlegm away.

I stood up and stretched, my body ached. I wouldn't be surprised if I had multiple bruises on my hips and shoulders.

"How did you sleep?" I asked Easton.

His hair was unrulier than I had ever seen it, and that was saying a lot.

"Um . . ." His voice was high enough to tell me it was no walk in the park for him either.

I chuckled. "One and done. Me too."

Easton laughed. I joined him on a small blanket next to the fire and examined my surroundings. Everything looked different in the light. The birds chirped near and far, and the lush green branches lifted and lowered with the gentle breeze.

"We didn't do marshmallows last night," I said.

"Let's have them with our coffee," Easton said before getting them out of the trunk of his car.

"Do you have skewers? Or should I find some sticks?" I called out to him.

"I've got skewers!"

Easton handed me everything I needed to make roasted marshmallows and then proceeded to pour our coffees. It was quiet until the caffeine brought me back to life.

"If you have time, I would like to show you a great spot. It's about a forty-minute hike," Easton said.

"Yeah, that sounds great. It's not like I have a job to get to or anything," I smiled.

We finished our coffee and marshmallows before taking down the tent. We packed the belongings into the back of Easton's trunk, and we set out on our hike. Being amongst nature with his kind soul was grounding. I soaked in everything: his gate, his laughter, and the way the sunlight lit his eyes into a trillion shards of crystal. I took in the green dragonfly that followed Easton like a lost puppy. I wanted to take every morsel of the memory with me so that when I took my last breath, I could come back here, and my heart could smile one last time.

We came upon a large clearing in the forest. One larger than life dead tree overlooked the Truly River before it bled into the New River. It was breathtaking. Easton held my hand and led me to the tree. We picked a spot nestled in its roots, which was large enough to make for excellent seating.

"It's beautiful. How did you find this place?" I asked.

Easton shrugged, "I've been here before," he said.

He was good at being vague. I wondered if he had come here with an ex-girlfriend, but if he had, I guess I wouldn't want to know. Or would I?

"Have you been in love before?" I asked, still unsure if I wanted to hear his answer.

Easton shot me a look of concern for my well-being. Huh. *Guess I shouldn't have asked.*

"I've loved before," he said, choosing his words carefully.

The dragonfly had returned and taken a particular interest in Easton. It must have been attracted to his scent. I couldn't blame it; I was too. Easton smiled like a child and watched as the insect fluttered around his face. The green exterior glimmered in the sunlight like a magical creature. I think I liked watching his wonder more than the oddity of the flying bug itself.

"Silly thing, isn't it?" I said.

"It's quite something," he replied.

I looked out to the river and watched as a flock of birds swooped down to the water and back up again.

"I wonder what it's like to fly. Do you think I'll get my wings when I die?" The flock soared over our heads.

"I don't know what I think. It's complicated, I guess. Maybe there are different options?" Easton said.

"Like what?"

"Oh, I don't know." Easton picked up a small stick and began to draw in the dirt.

Sometimes it was like pulling teeth to get him to talk. I only wanted to know what he thought.

"You know, there's no right or wrong answer. Sometimes I wonder if blackness is the best option. As much as I fear it, I think I fear the regrets more. You taught me that!" I flicked a pebble at him.

"Hey! That wasn't my intention. I don't want you to worry; I just want to help you make the right decisions." Easton picked the pebble off of his jacket and tossed it aside.

"Easton?" I asked in sincerity.

"Yeah?"

"I love you," I said, not wanting any more regrets. His face softened, and his eyes lit from within.

"I love you too, Beck." Easton placed a hand over his heart before leaning over and showing me with a soft and long kiss. He pulled away with a smile so content that I could stay in the moment forever.

"I don't want you to hide anything from me. I know you said I don't know you. But I do! I know the impact that you have made on my heart. And there's nothing you can say that will change that." I took a deep breath, "Do you believe me?"

"Come on Beck, that's not fair," Easton said.

"What's not?"

He sighed in exasperation. No words followed.

"You're afraid that I won't love you after you tell me. Do you know what I'm afraid of?" I asked.

Easton looked at me, afraid of what I might say. I saw in his eyes that my fear was the chink in his armor.

"I'm afraid that the one I love won't let me in. I'm afraid our relationship will be stunted, and there's not a damn thing I can do about it," I said, not realizing how I felt until I said it.

I understood all my anger from before. Blanketed under this simple statement. It was lack of control that I feared most. I couldn't control my health, how Easton felt, or if he wanted to open up to me.

Easton considered my words. His eyes squinted in the sun and his laugh lines deepened in the absence of humor.

"Are you afraid of dying?" Easton asked before he looked over the river.

"Of course, I am. Who wouldn't be?" I said.

"I was too. The first time I died."

$\mathcal{I}$ whipped my head to Easton and observed him carefully as he built the courage to continue. My mind raced from medical conditions to accidents, but nothing prepared me for what he said next.

"I would like to say that practice makes perfect, but that's not the case when it comes to death. Sure, it gets easier with time, as many things do, but perfect is an unachievable goal for the human race."

His words flowed like the melody of a sweet song, but he was singing in a different language—one I didn't understand.

I watched his face contort with the pain that only life on earth could offer. He momentarily took the break he needed before continuing down a slow path to honesty. I knew it was my time to listen, and I tried my damn hardest not to judge him for what he believed to be his truth.

"I'm what's called a Tethered Soul, Beck." Easton's gaze dropped down to the dirt before him. He looked as broken as the day I met him. "No matter how many times I die, my soul returns."

I sucked in a quick breath when he finally looked at me. His irises, electric blue, were flanked by bolts of red.

"I've lived a dozen lives over the years. It never ends for me. I'm like a prisoner." Easton broke our contact and looked back over the river. A single tear fell from his eye.

I knew Easton had been hiding something, but I didn't expect it to be this. I didn't know how to react. I felt stupid for believing him, but I did. He was my proof, sitting right there in front of me. He was no normal man. He was an old soul, and now I knew why he remained so comfortable in his own skin.

Easton continued. "In all my lives, I've never loved someone like you. You're it for me. And when you pass on to another dimension in time . . . I'll remain. A new place, a new family, but I will *always* . . . have the same broken heart, and the same damn tethered soul."

Easton ran his hands through his hair, and the tears flowed effortlessly. I mindlessly rubbed the knot in my throat as I struggled to put the pieces together. He would have to feed me more because right now, I only saw the tip of the iceberg. And there was a lot yet to uncover.

"Say something! Anything!" Easton pled.

I didn't know what to say. I was stunned, unable to form complete thoughts, let alone a comprehensible sentence.

"I love you."

It was the one thing I knew to be true. My whole life was upside down. I didn't know right from wrong or up from down, but I knew that I loved Easton Green. No matter how many lives he lived. Or believed he had.

I moved over to Easton and sat as close as I could, resting my head on his shoulder. I wasn't quite sure what was happening, but I was there for him either way.

"So, I'm sorry. I'm just trying to get it all straight. You've lived . . . *multiple* lives?" It felt as dumb to say aloud as it did to hear it.

Easton responded as if it were an everyday conversation about the weather. Only, this time, he was personally affected by the storm.

"Twelve or thirteen, probably. I lost count."

"Thirteen!" I said, sitting up to look at his face. He looked away as if he were ashamed.

I scrambled to my feet.

"Don't go!" Easton cried out.

I took a deep breath, "I'm not! I'm um, I'm just trying to come to grips with what you're telling me. That's all." I shook out my hands and began to pace.

Easton stood and dusted the dirt off his pants.

"Let's walk," he said.

"Yeah." I agreed. I needed something to do with my arms and legs. I needed moving parts and the passing scenery. I needed to understand.

"I know, it's a lot to take in."

I laughed out loud. I tried to stop for fear it was coming off as rude, but my nerves wouldn't allow for it.

"It's not that I don't believe you. I do! I just . . . I'm having a hard time understanding," I said as I interlocked my hands in weird and uncomfortable formations.

"OK! I can help with that!" Easton was excited about the development of my reaction. It was something he could work with, and as I told him before, I wasn't going anywhere.

"You have memories of when you were a kid, right?" he asked.

I nodded.

"Like two years old, three years old?"

"Sure . . ."

"OK, I do too! But I have them with different families, all around the world."

"What!?" I stopped walking.

He was explaining it well, but my heart was still picking up speed.

"It's true. I'm always me. My soul, my memory, my personality. Always. But my situation is different. My adopted parents, siblings, the country, the lifestyle: that changes every time. I've grown to adapt. I've learned to read people—understand them. I know what makes this world turn and understand motive more than anyone you will ever meet. I've learned it all from experience." Easton ran his hand through his hair and gave me a hopeful expression.

"So . . . . I'm sorry! I don't know what to ask! I'm so confused! Who are you now? Who were you then? Are you even a construction sales rep—"

"I am Easton Green. And I love you, more than any soul I've ever met! If you let me love you, I will show you the greatest love of a lifetime. Everly, please don't give up on me!" Easton stilled and squeezed my hand tightly.

My heart melted, and my body slacked.

"I don't fully understand Easton, but I wasn't lying when I said there was nothing you could say to change my mind. And if this is your reality, I want to know about it. Count me in. Always."

I hugged him, pressing my ear up to his beating heart. *Lub-dub, lub-dub, lub-dub.* I held on until I felt I was beginning to digest the gravity of what Easton had told me.

"So, you are or aren't a construction sales rep?" I joked.

Easton smiled but wasn't ready to laugh.

"You got me! I'm not a sales rep."

"I knew it! I knew it!" I shouted and pulled away to push his chest playfully.

This time he laughed at my excitement. "How did you know?"

"Your hands are too soft!"

Easton examined his hands, "What? Are you saying I have girly hands?"

I laughed off the tension, and we continued to poke fun of each other. Our walk back to the car consisted of me trying to pick out which morsels of information he fed me were fact and which were fiction.

So far, it'd been my favorite game yet. It was better than any game I obsessed over as a child. I learned that he didn't have a job; he never needed one with his investment knowledge and maturity to invest young. Though that never stopped him from getting a job he wanted. I learned that he did have a family, albeit adopted. He cared for them but said that only a few select people left an impression on him and that sometimes it was easier not to get attached. I learned that his last life was stationed in sunny California, where he spent his days surfing and being a beach bum. It was a real shame that he couldn't bring his tan with him.

When we got back into his car, I was pleased to see Easton take out the Hunter's to-go menu from his glovebox. He crossed off camping before folding it back up into a neat square again.

CHAPTER 18

*P*earl buttons lined the sheer opening of Chloe's back. It was a lot of skin to show, but she was comfortable with that, and I would rather see her back than her chest. Unfortunately, I saw that too. Her cleavage popped out of the sweetheart line dress as she continued to pull on it. The gown trailed to the floor and pooled beyond her feet. It was a beautiful dress. I nodded in agreement with my mom and Chloe's mother and grandmother.

It was sweet that she invited me, and I felt myself opening up to the possibility that she might not be as bad as I originally thought. We all had deep dark secrets, after all; what if hers was that she was secretly awesome? Far-fetched, but possible.

Chloe clapped, and both our mothers mimicked her enthusiasm with the same applause. Her grandmother smiled a toothless grin from her wheelchair.

"OK, but I still think it's a toss-up between this one and number two!" Chloe announced.

"Pumpkin, *this* is the one!" her mother said.

"Really?" Chloe said in a tone that could call a wolf pack home.

Chloe's mom nodded her head, and the tears began to fall. It was an emotional moment for them. Chloe trotted to her mom in her heels that were too high and too big, and they embraced, both crying and speaking in dolphin.

It was hard for me to be excited for her when I knew I would never have a wedding of my own. I wasn't even sure I would make it to their wedding. I felt my secret growing larger by the day. It was like a black cloud that followed me everywhere I went. Only I knew the severity of the storm ahead.

"That's going to be you one day," Mom whispered in my ear. I frowned—nothing like rubbing salt in the wounds.

"OK, enough of that! Everly, try on your bridesmaid dress?" Chloe asked.

"Huh?"

I was horrified. The last thing I wanted to do was put on a purple satin gown and show off how ridiculous I looked to a group of people. But apparently, Chloe didn't have close friends—it was a major red flag—so, when she asked me to be her maid of honor, I had to comply. It was probably my best acting yet.

A saleswoman with beady eyes ushered me to a dressing room where the purple dress hung waiting for me. I couldn't tell if it was her tiny eyes or that she was judging me for my lack of excitement and loyalty to the bride. I closed the door and sighed, giving myself a small moment of pity before making a fool of myself.

After dressing, I checked myself out from every angle I could. The tri-fold mirrors made it easy, and every angle I saw I hated. I never found myself to be girly. Dresses looked awkward on me at best. My knees were too knobby, my hips too straight. I looked like a thirteen-year-old boy in a nightgown. And what's worse? I had to stand on a miniature stage and have four women judge me on it. I gave the mirror one last distraught look before I met my fate.

"It's a pretty dress, but I don't know if I can do it justice. My hips just—"

"I love it!" Chloe squealed, sealing the deal.

"I do, too!" I lied.

I was pretty sure only the grandma caught on. Well, her and Miss Judgmental Eyes. My cheeks turned red under the scrutiny, and my shoulders slumped in defeat while the tailor pulled, pinched, and pinned my dress.

"Honey, you look like you're losing weight!" my mom said.

"No, I don't think so."

"What's your secret?" Chloe asked, and the room lightened up. "I've been mowing down celery like it's going out of style! But I'm only two pounds away from my wedding shred weight! I think I can do it!" Chloe checked herself out in the mirror.

I was relieved when I was dressed in my clothes again. Jeans and a hooded sweatshirt: nothing was more comfortable than that combination. I prayed I wouldn't have to wear the purple dress for an entire evening. The thought of standing in front of all the guests wearing nothing but a thin satin draping freaked me out—enough to wonder if I could call out sick and leave Chloe at the altar with no backup. I wouldn't do it, of course, but that didn't mean it wasn't tempting.

The five of us went to lunch after the fitting. It was a cute café, wrought iron tables lined the sidewalk, and I was able to people watch instead of engaging in conversation. Each person that passed, I wondered if they were a Tethered Soul like Easton, and I imagined what kinds of lives they had lived in the past.

"How are things going with your boyfriend, Everly?" Chloe asked.

I jumped when I heard my name, snapping back to reality. *Boyfriend?* I suppose it was true. Easton was my boyfriend now. I liked the way it sounded.

"It's good!"

"Ohhh, look at that! She's getting embarrassed!" my mom cooed.

Drawing attention to it only made it worse. If I was pink before, I was red now.

"Mom!" I tried, but my attempt failed.

"I've never seen her this smitten by a boy before! Not even Evan Styles! The boy she pined after for two years and they went to homecoming together! I thought she had it bad then, but now? Wooo . . ." Mom fanned her face, and I rolled my eyes.

"Evan was just a fling, Mom." I looked to the other women. "It was nothing. Don't listen to her."

"Do you love him?"

It was a bold question coming from Chloe. I couldn't believe that she would pry like that in front of our mothers and her grandma. But before I could think of something clever to answer, all the women, including the grandma, made all sorts of high pitch squeals. I cursed my God-given face for deceiving me in the way that it did.

"Ohhh, I remember my first love . . ." Chloe's grandmother said.

"Yeah, Grams married my grandpa super young. They were high school sweethearts!" Chloe announced.

"Aw, that's so sweet!" My mom placed a hand over her heart.

"Just because that geezer was my last love doesn't mean he was my first!" Chloe's grandma spit through her missing teeth.

It was the best thing I'd heard all day. I loved a senior with an attitude. I sat up straight in my chair, eager to listen to her story. After the waiter took our menus, she began.

"Two boys were fighting over me my first year in high school. Frank and Harold."

"Frank is my grandpa," Chloe added.

I loved it already.

"Frank was handsome, but nobody held a candle to Harold. He was a bad boy, he lived on the wrong side of the tracks, and I loved him more than anything. We used to sneak around so my parents wouldn't find out."

"Grandma!" Chloe said.

"My parents were friends with Frank's parents. They were a good family. Hard-working. I liked Frank well enough, but he was no Harold. When my parents found out I was fooling around with that boy, they forbade me to see him."

"What did you do?" I muttered.

"Oh, I had to listen to them. They'd whip my butt with a belt if I didn't. Lash my tush until it bled! You can't do that these days. They'd think you're a bad parent. Abusive, they'd say."

I chuckled and found myself wondering how old Easton's views dated back. I briefly pondered if he valued waiting until marriage before having sex. I winced, remembering when he turned me down in the tent. I was thankful when Chloe's grandma continued with her lisp-ridden story of forbidden love.

"After a while of Frank trying to get to know me, I caved. There's only so much will power a young girl has, and I was bored. I started to go out with him to help me get over Harold. And eventually, I did."

"But Grams, you love Grandpa, don't you?" Chloe asked.

"Oh yeah, I love the crusty geezer. It took years for it to grow through. Some love is meant to be. Some love . . . well, you can make it work."

Chloe and her mother were visibly disturbed by her confession. Although from Chloe's mother's expression, I imagined she'd heard the story before. I was sure I was the only one who thoroughly enjoyed the grandmother's confession. It struck true for me too. And I took pleasure in the idea that I had chosen my Harold.

The five of us continued our lunch. My panini was

delicious, but my appetite only allowed for a small portion. I took the leftovers home with me in a box. It would make for a good dinner. All and all, the day wasn't too bad. I began to look at Chloe as a Frank. Maybe it was a love that wasn't instant or true, but it had the potential to work regardless. I hoped for my brother's sake that their love was a hidden Harold.

I would have met Easton at Fresh Grounds, but I was too embarrassed to show my face. I told him to meet me in the parking lot across the street instead.

I called Lindsay and told her all about the romantic night camping Easton had put together for me. I left out the part where he may or may not be a mad man. The jury was out, but I loved him nonetheless. It sure did make for some interesting conversation, and I was thankful to have a new focus. I promised Lindsay I would still come into the coffee shop, but she had to tell me who would be on the schedule first. I didn't need the wrath of Jacob.

When Easton jumped in my truck, he gave me a quick peck on the cheek.

"What's the secret mission?" he asked.

I had something that I needed to do. Due diligence, if you will. But I was slightly ashamed of myself for it. That's why I needed backup.

"Do you remember that girl we saw at Hunters?" I asked.

"No. I don't remember a girl. However, I do remember

you making a young man feel as small as a boy when you pointed out that his shirt was missing buttons. Was the girl before that, or after that?"

I shot Easton a look. He held up his palms, "Joking! I was joking!" he said, before mumbling under his breath, "True story though . . ."

"Hope, the girl on the date. She was the one I wanted my brother to marry," I said.

"Oh, yeah, I remember. What about her?"

"I went to Chloe's dress fitting today, and I'm having a hard time accepting that she's the right one for my brother. I just want to talk to Hope. Do a little sleuthing," I said like a true Clover girl.

Easton was apprehensive. I could tell he disapproved of me meddling in their relationship.

"I don't know how to say this, Beck—"

"Just say it!"

"I think you should trust your brother and respect his decisions. You don't know his heart."

Easton made a good point.

"I know his mind! And I know he's attracted to shiny new things! And I know that when the newness of their relationship fades, he's going to wish he'd picked someone with more depth. But it'll be too late then! He'll have a baby! I know my brother, and he's making the wrong decision! Hope is the manager at the supermarket; I'm just going to talk—"

"I have an idea!" Easton interrupted. "Before you talk to Hope, why don't you talk to your brother?"

I frowned.

"Have you ever talked to him about this?"

"No," I admitted.

"Out of respect, I think he should be your first stop. Then, maybe even Chloe. And a far, distant third, Hope. And maybe not even then . . ."

I threw myself back in my seat under protest. He was right, as usual.

"So, no Hope?"

"No Hope."

"Come with me to talk to my brother?" I asked Easton. He was pleased with the new direction, and we were on our way.

It was a Wednesday, and I knew my brother would be working. We went to K & C's Concrete, and it didn't take long for me to find him.

"Hey, Dork! What brings you here?" Carter said, eyeing Easton and me.

"Hey, do you have a second to chat?" I asked.

"Now? Is everything OK?" he asked. It made my stomach turn.

"I just wanted to talk to you about the wedding. That's all."

"Oh, OK. I'm due for a break. I'll meet you at the benches by the deli in five," Carter said before heading back inside.

I squeezed Easton's hand, thankful he was by my side. My brother and I didn't have conversations beyond name-calling, but it didn't mean I didn't care.

I sat with my back toward the fading sun. A little warmth hit my back, but it wasn't enough. A shudder ripped through me. I couldn't tell if I was cold or incredibly apprehensive. Was I doing the right thing? I wanted to pull out, but it was too late. Carter sat down opposite me.

"So, what brings you here? You never come to my work!" Carter said with a less than welcoming tone.

"I . . ." I looked at Easton, my eyes begging for help. He placed his hand on my knee and squeezed. But that's all he offered. He was going to make me do this all on my own. I deserved as much.

"I wanted to give you my blessing!" I couldn't believe it when the words came out of my mouth, and by the looks of my brother, he didn't either. I was too scared to say what I actually thought.

Carter took off his sunglasses and squinted into the sunlight.

"Look Beck, I know you don't like her, but you don't see who she is when we're alone," he said.

"No! I know!" It was something I'd just realized in that moment.

"She's kind, and she cares a lot about other people. She's a good person. And she doesn't show it all the time, but she's deeper than you'd know."

"Totally!" I nodded, never doubting him for a moment.

"She's incredibly insecure. You wouldn't know it by looking at her, cause she's hot as hell, but it comes out all weird. Lots of makeup, showy clothes, an over-the-top personality. But when she's with me and we're home on the couch, and she's got no makeup, and my old baggy t-shirt on; that's the woman I chose to marry. Just give her a chance, Beck. You'll like her." Carter glared at me, part pleading, part warning.

"No! Yeah! I get it! I'm here for you, and I can't wait to get to know her better. She's going to make a great addition to our family," I said, feeling no better than scum.

Thank God, I never went to Hope!

Carter put his sunglasses back on and stood up. I guess we were done talking.

"Wait!" I blurted out. No regrets. "It wasn't Chloe; she was never the problem. It's me. Nobody will ever be good enough for you, in my eyes. I'm sorry I ever doubted your decision."

For the first time, I watched my brother look at Easton with a softening of his eyes. Approving almost. He knew Easton was right for me, too. Besides, it was likely that my feelings about Chloe were similar to his own for Easton and the confession resonated all the more for that reason. Carter nodded and slapped Easton on the back before heading back to work. And when he was out of sight, I refused to look at Easton's "I told you so" face.

CHAPTER 19

"I know you want to say it," I said.

Easton held up both his hands, saying nothing. *Smart boy.*

"If you're not going to say it, I will. You were right. I had no business meddling in my brother's relationship. How could I have been so blind?" I asked, mostly thinking aloud, but more than interested in knowing if Easton had an answer.

"When you're emotionally invested, it's easy to have your judgment clouded," Easton said. He was too kind.

"Yeah, but your judgment's never off. You always know best. You knew today when I wanted to talk to Hope." I prepared to go on and on, but Easton cut me off.

"And that took a very, very long time to figure out, though. It can be difficult still, and I'm sure I'll continue to make mistakes. I'm not perfect." Easton shrugged. "We're human," he said.

"You are?"

"I am what?"

"Human?" I asked.

Easton's face fell. "Seriously?"

"What!? I've never met a . . . a . . ." I waved my hands about in the air. I didn't know where I was going with this, but it sounded worse the longer it continued. "I don't know, OK? I don't know what you are." I sank in my seat.

"I'm a human, as are you," Easton said.

I rolled my eyes. "Well, last time I checked, we don't come back from the dead, so—"

"What, do you think I'm a zombie?" Easton was beginning to find it humorous. I was too exhausted.

"Look, I'm sorry. I've had a long day. They made me try on this awful purple dress, and then I got spit on by this toothless grandma . . ."

"What? Really?"

"Yeah, actually, she was amazing. The spitting, not so much."

"Why don't you come over for some dinner? We can watch a movie?" Easton offered.

"I would love that, but I have to get back to Yeti. I don't have it in me to stay out late." Too bad, because I was dying to see his place. No pun intended.

"I'll come to yours then."

"Really? I'd love that, as long as you don't mind me being so tired?" I wanted to spend all my hours with him, but I was still exhausted from camping. It had been a couple of days ago, but I was dragging, nonetheless.

"You go home, get on pajamas, and I'll pick up dinner

and bring it over," Easton said. It was nice not to have to plan anything.

"That sounds great," I said.

When I got home, I spent my time picking up the breakfast plate that I left on the kitchen counter and the random socks that Yeti had stolen and dispersed throughout the house. I had just enough time to brush my teeth before the doorbell rang.

"Hi, come on in. Um, sorry about the . . ." I motioned towards the pile of shoes by the front door. There would be other things that I would be embarrassed about too, but I had to let it go if I wanted to enjoy my time with Easton.

"I hope you like Mexican food?" Easton held up a bag from the only Mexican restaurant in Clover.

"It's my favorite!" I said.

I felt a little awkward with Easton in my house. It was a funny thing that happened to the mind. My insecurities about the cleanliness, lack of décor, and absent furnishings— no matter how insignificant—still overpowered everything else that had happened in our relationship. All the while, he'd recently told me his deepest darkest secret, and it was beyond any fear of a messy kitchen. I felt the insecurities all the same. I was eager to look past it all and get to a place where we were entirely comfortable with each other.

"I want to see your place; I'm curious where you live," I said as I pulled out paper plates and real silverware.

"I'd like that too. But, don't have high expectations. It's nothing fancy."

I pointed around my kitchen. The original cabinetry

from the eighties, the stained grout between the white tiles, and the one attempt I'd made at a decoration: a chicken statue. Easton smiled and cocked his head to the side.

"Are there others like you?" I asked, suddenly curious if there could be another him out there.

I watched his face contort as I mindlessly unwrapped the food. Easton took a seat at the kitchen island.

"There are. Not many, I suppose. I've only met a few dozen or so."

"Really? A few dozen?"

"Yeah, um, remember the homeless man outside of the bar?" Easton's face softened with what I assumed was empathy, maybe sadness.

"Nooo!" I said, drawing out the word.

Easton chuckled, "Yeah, that's Simon. He's all but given up. It's a hard life, and I understand why many choose to drown themselves in drugs and alcohol. They're just trying to escape." Easton plated a chicken burrito and doused it in salsa.

It was sad to me too. I never looked past Simon's dirty face. It was becoming a theme in my life—one I'd like to nip. I had so much to learn but so little time.

"He called you something; it was like he knew you . . ."

"Sam?"

"Yeah!"

"The first time we met, my name was Sam. That's what he'll always remember me as," Easton said.

"You get a different name each time?" I asked before taking a bite of my dinner.

"I'm always adopted under the same name. Half of my

parents honor my given name—It's Easton Green, by the way—and half of them change it, sometimes using a variation similar to the original and sometimes changing it altogether. I used to care and legally change my name back the second I turned of age. I don't care so much anymore."

"Wow." I took a moment to let it sink in: multiple lives, multiple names.

"But how did Simon know that you were like him?" I asked, intrigued. I could probably ask questions all night and still not finish.

Easton worked to clear the food in his mouth, holding a napkin over his lips while he chewed.

"Sorry, there's just so much to understand." I apologized for the interrogation; it wasn't very hospitable of me.

"No, don't be sorry. I like it. I've never been able to talk to someone about this before—"

"You've never told anyone!?" I blurted out.

"I have—a couple of times. Um, I've told one of my best friends before. It didn't end well. And I've told a few parents, all in my early lives. Every time, I regretted it. The worst was when I was put under psychiatric care," Easton said with a shrug.

My jaw dropped. "But you took a chance telling me," I stated.

"I did." Easton put his food down for a moment of reflection.

"Why?"

"God, I knew it was going to go one of two ways. I was so scared, and every life experience I had was telling me not to." Easton shook his head and stared off into the distance.

"What changed your mind?"

Easton's focus came back to me. "I couldn't stunt your chance at love. If you chose to leave me, that would be a valid decision, but I didn't have the right to make that decision for you."

"Thank you for giving me a choice." I smiled at him, realizing that he'd given me a choice, and I wasn't as stripped of control as I previously thought.

We finished our dinner. The conversation flowed effortlessly, even in my exhausted state. Easton picked a movie about a man able to travel through time. It was no wonder why he proclaimed it as one of his favorites. He lay on the sofa, and I crawled in front of him, careful not to block his view. No matter how mind-bending or heartbreaking the movie may have been, I was never going to last. I fell asleep in Easton's arms. My guess would have been in the first five minutes.

I felt more at home in Easton's arms than I ever had in my house alone. And while his arms kept the terror away, I still dreamed of death. At the very least, I was unconscious when the dream played out like a movie; it was much better than being awake and gouging out the backs of my arms and threatening the life of my cell phone. But, even though I was asleep during this particular dream, it still took up residency in my mind the same as a memory would. And I was disappointed when I awoke with a memory of drowning to death. The nightmares hardly seemed fair. I had enough horror to deal with in my real life, and I didn't need it in my sleep too.

The despair drained from my memory when my eyes

focused on Easton. He sat in the recliner, reading a book and sipping coffee from Fresh Grounds. The sunlight brushing the side of his face. I was pleased to see that he had stayed the night.

"Good morning," Easton said, taking me in.

"Good morning."

"I brought you a coffee. Thankfully, Lindsay was working, and she knew your order. I think she left you a little note on your coffee sleeve." Easton held out my coffee.

The note read, "Call me!" I read her message aloud and chuckled. I'd been neglecting her and my family. I knew it wasn't right, but it was the easiest path for me at the moment. I missed her.

"I see you found the blankets." I lifted the blanket he had draped over me. I had a small stack of throw blankets in a cupboard tucked away in the hall.

"I didn't snoop, I—"

"No, it's fine. Thank you. And thank you for the coffee." I rarely had coffee upon waking. It was nice.

"Did you sleep OK? I thought about moving you to your bed, but I didn't want to wake you. You seemed . . . restless," Easton said.

"Oh, I slept fine. It was just a dream, but . . . um, actually, I slept better than I have in a while. I think it's because you were here."

Easton smiled, and I blushed. I hid behind my coffee cup.

"You know, the house gets lonely. And the quieter it gets, the louder my thoughts become."

Easton nodded without saying anything. Sometimes it was nice just to know somebody understood.

"Well, I've got to head out. I have some errands to run. Are you going to be OK today?" Easton closed his book and placed it under his arm.

"Oh! Yeah," I shook my head. Why wouldn't I be OK? I had stuff to do too. Like sleep.

"You should call Lindsay. I know it's hard, but I think it would be good for both of you to spend a little time catching up. It seemed like she missed you." Easton smiled before turning to leave.

"Yeah, maybe I will," I muttered. He had always been right in the past; I'm sure this was no exception.

Dear Lindsay, I wrote.

I didn't call her. Nor did I visit. But I did take a nap, and I was productively writing my goodbye to Lindsay. It was hard work. Draining work. By the end of the letter, I'd need a hot shower to wash away the emotion.

I told her why she was my best friend, and I shared my most hilarious and treasured memories with her. And I told her why I was too much of a coward to talk to her in person. I asked for forgiveness, and I begged her not to feel sad. I wrote my wish that she would only remember me with a smile.

The day had come and gone when I caught wind that Chloe was having a bachelorette party the following weekend. For an introvert such as myself, a bachelorette party was a dreaded event. The thought of pretending to have something in common with a bunch of ladies on a party bus sounded horrendous. Nonetheless, I committed myself to give it my best shot. I owed it to Carter for doubting him. And to be honest, I was a little intrigued to get to know the real Chloe—the one that Carter knew and loved.

CHAPTER 20

So, what did you say you were going to school for?" I asked the girl next to me.

I'd already forgotten her name. She had a short pixie cut and cute freckles. I wanted to call her Alice, but I knew that wasn't right. I wouldn't chance it.

"Um—" she started.

"Suck it!" The crazy one yelled to the one with long blond hair and a penis straw.

The limo bounced, and I tried to hold on to the leather seats. It was uber hot, and the six of us ladies had packed in tight like sardines. The smell of alcohol permeated the air, and I was thankful you couldn't get drunk off the smell alone. I was taking it easy. I had a weak stomach, I said. It wasn't entirely untrue.

"Um, I'm just taking general ed classes. I don't know what I want to do yet," not Alice, said.

I nodded. It was so awkward when the conversation died. Now I had to do all sorts of work to come up with other questions. I picked up my cell phone as if I had a notification ping that only I could hear. I scrolled through several apps, buying myself time before having to talk to someone again. Chloe was the only one I knew—and not well either. I was hoping we would have some time to get to know each other, but by the looks of the half-empty tequila bottle, and the still setting sun, tonight was going to be a long one and not for talking.

At some point, maybe I could sneak out early. I wouldn't be missed. That was for sure. The five girls all knew each other from high school, and one of them, as early as elementary. They had all sorts of inside jokes and a plethora of things to talk about. I was the only newcomer. And I was not open to making new friends. Quite the opposite, actually. I was in the market for downgrading. Saying goodbye and closing the door. I shouldn't have come.

I texted Easton. I prayed he would tell me to hold tight and that he would bail me out. He didn't. He was overly optimistic that I would find some fun by the end of the night. I threw my head back and braced myself for another bump; then, I spent all of my energy on joining the party. I started with a shot.

By the time we got to the karaoke bar, I was feeling sick to my stomach. I didn't know if it was my condition or not, but I hadn't been able to consume alcohol the way I used to. Each and every time, my tolerance would shrink. I knew I shouldn't have had any, but I wanted desperately to rid myself of my social awkwardness that came with being an introvert and the burden I carried of keeping a secret with the magnitude of cancer.

We stammered out of the limo. All of us had penis headbands, except for Chloe. She had a crown, a sash, and a ball and chain around her ankle. It was degrading at best. Everyone stopped and stared. I wished I was intoxicated enough not to notice, but I wasn't. I was on the cusp of being chattier but also starting to yawn at an accelerated rate. I was ready for bed, and it couldn't be later than seven.

The girls tumbled into the bar. I lagged behind. Something was off; it was either motion sickness or déjà vu. I stopped altogether on the curb as the others disappeared into the karaoke bar. I saw something I recognized. But what? I looked around the busy streets. A car honked as a guy hung out the back window with his phone. Was I a celebrity? No, I had a penis on my head. I snatched the hideous headband off of my head and hid it under my jacket. My stomach churned in humility. I was safer with the pack.

It was then, when I made my decision to head inside, that I saw him.

There, across the street, tucked behind the trash cans, was Simon. Like a hidden gem. I knew I recognized something, and it was his dog that came out to greet us when we unloaded from the limo—looking for scraps, no doubt. I crossed the street, thankful I no longer was getting the attention from onlookers, and came upon Simon sleeping on top of newspapers. His sign was different this time: "Need Help to Feed Family." Poor guy. It was his only hope; he probably changed it out all the time, testing it like an advertisement. Seeing what sticks can be hard work. I knew that from my design classes at the college.

"Simon?" I said.

He was out cold. His clothes were so dirty that they were nearly black, and the deep wrinkles in his face showed pale against the dirt on his skin. His hair was so greasy, I wondered when the last time he had a proper shower. I stood above him—his dog whimpering—and I wondered what I could do to help this Tethered Soul.

"Simon!?"

I forced out a louder call, but my voice cracked. It'd been doing that a lot lately. I rubbed at my neck. The little dog begged at my feet, and I just stood there helplessly. The least I could do was give him a proper meal. Maybe the smell of hot food would wake him.

There was a taco shop two blocks down, if I recalled correctly. I made my way there and ordered five rolled tacos with guacamole and sour cream. I was back in no time, and Simon had woken up naturally. He sat, back hunched against the wall of a steakhouse. It was probably prime picking when they brought out the leftovers. I'm sure his dog loved it as well.

"Simon?" I said again.

Simon's eyes widened at the sight of me and then dropped to the container of food. His dog stood on two legs and danced.

"I know you probably don't remember me, but I'm Beck. I'm East—Sam's friend." I corrected myself.

Simon nodded. It was a brief encounter, and it was dark, I didn't blame him for not remembering me in his drunken state.

"I brought you some food. Are you hungry?" I asked as I sat down beside him.

"Yeah!"

Simon took the food, his eyes large in wonder. He tore into a rolled taco. But no matter how hungry that man was, he still had the loyalty to share with his dog. Simon gave him one full taco. It was a generous gift. As if that wasn't enough to melt my heart, he offered me one next.

"Oh!" I waved my hands about, "No, thank you, I've got to get back to a thing."

Simon looked at me with questioning eyes.

"Yeah, my brother's getting married, so I'm here with his fiancée, celebrating." I pulled the penis headband out from my jacket and gave it a little shake.

Simon began to laugh; a toothless smile spread across his face, and I laughed with him.

"There! Over there!" Chloe yelled to the crazy one. Her long arm pointed at me from across the street.

Shit.

"Looks like the penis sisters found me!" I said to Simon, and we laughed some more.

The girls crossed the street, "What are you doing out here, Everly? We've been looking all over for you!" Chloe said.

"Yeah! We looked in the bathroom. Twice!" the crazy one said.

I rolled my eyes. Not on purpose. It was natural.

"OK, yeah, I'll be right there," I said, not wanting to

leave the wisdom tucked within this homeless man. He was like a unicorn that only I could see.

The girls exchanged shifty glances.

"Like, let's go then. Now." Chloe had *hero* written all over her face. She would later tell the story as if she saved me from the dangerous homeless man.

I sighed and looked over to Simon. "Do you like to sing?" I asked.

The girls began to whisper. At least, they thought they were whispering. Simon chuckled and pointed to his chest.

"Yeah! Come with us! More food and drinks too!" I said.

Simon was quick to his feet. The girls were apprehensive—that was until the crazy one screamed.

"Wooooooo! Partaaayyyy!" She thrust her arms in the air as if she'd just won a boxing match and ran across the street. More cars honked, and Chloe ran after her, her legs pinned at the knees. I knew that run. The girl had to pee. I crossed the street slower than the girls before me, remaining at Simon's side. He was a stiff man, and I assumed sleeping on the concrete would do that to the young and old alike.

The karaoke bar was loud for being at half capacity. The night was early, and I was thankful we got in when we did. Our party was by far the most obnoxious. Even worse than the woman singing "My Heart Will Go On." I was embarrassed for her. She was most likely in her early forties, and she was not here to party. No, this woman was serious; she probably came here after work to fill the void of never becoming a professional singer. When she stretched out her voice, it was clear why this had never taken off for her. She felt it deep within her and looked like she might cry at the sound of her own vocals. Others might cry for a different reason. It was hard to watch.

The waitress got an extra seat for Simon. Most of the girls were taken aback by his presence, but the girl not named Alice gave me an approving smile.

"Hi, I'm Audrey."

Audrey! I knew it wasn't Alice!

"Hi."

Simon gave her a toothless grin. He was so happy, and I felt grateful that I was able to brighten his day. It was fate that our paths crossed, and I was glad I came. Easton was right *again.* I did find a patch of happiness on this bachelorette night.

Simon ordered the kitchen sink and two shots of bourbon. When his food came, I ended up taking one of his shots with him. You only live once! Well, not Simon. He lived a lot.

"To Simon, and the amazing life he's had the opportunity to live."

I held out my shot glass, and the five other girls did the same. Bourbon, vodka, two Sex on the Beaches, and one dirty martini joined forces for a brief moment in the middle of the table to celebrate Simon's life. It was nothing short of a miracle.

The night was a blast. I admittedly spent some of it throwing up in the bathroom, but that was only because my tolerance was zilch. Chloe showed us that she had somewhat of a decent singing voice, and at one point in the night, the crazy one showed us that she was wearing a neon pink bra. Simon got on stage to sing after some coaxing from the other five girls and me, and we all sang "Livin' on a Prayer." I only knew the chorus; Simon didn't know any of it. But that didn't stop us from singing our hearts out. It was a night I needed. And I was grateful.

When the time had come to say goodbye, I left Simon with all the cash I had in my purse, as Easton had. It wasn't much—sixty dollars perhaps—but he was touched. I said goodbye to Simon's dog and finished up with a tight squeeze around Simon's neck.

"Take care," I whispered.

The five girls said goodbye to Simon, giving him high fives, and pats on the back, thanking him for singing with us on stage. Simon beamed like a new man. I wondered if I'd ever see him again.

I felt good on the ride home. Tired beyond belief, but happy. I never got my time with Chloe, but Simon was an unexpected surprise that made my night worth the exertion. Something about being in the presence of an old soul made me feel grounded like I was one with nature. And Mother Nature was a beautiful thing.

CHAPTER 21

I was already half asleep by the time the limo dropped me off. I threw my shoes into the shoe graveyard and padded barefoot to the kitchen. I forced myself to drink a full glass of water before bed. My full belly made me feel even more nauseous, and I ended up throwing it up no more than five minutes later. I must have been really down on myself because Easton answered a text I didn't remember writing and came over to help. I knew enough to know I was embarrassed and that texting him was probably a mistake.

Easton was nothing less than a saint, though. He tied my hair into a ponytail and fetched me water. When I settled into bed after a hot shower, I begged him to stay. He didn't hesitate. He crawled into bed with me, and I was thankful for the warmth of his body. I nestled my face into his neck.

"What did you do tonight?" I mumbled into the darkness. His hair smelled of cherry cigars.

"I played poker tonight."

"Did I ever tell you I ran into your grandpa?" I fumbled on my words as I remembered the odd exchange I had with Clyde.

"You saw Clyde?" Easton asked.

"Yeah," I said, partially aware that I was incriminating myself.

"Where?" Easton's tone was confused. Possibly suspicious.

"Oh. Um." My eyes searched the black void of my room, worried about how he might take my stalkery, "At that bar, the one you took me to."

"You went to the bar? When?"

I took a deep breath. "I went when we weren't talking. I think I was trying to run into you. I missed you," I said. After what seemed like an eternity, I blurted out, "I was stalking you, OK?" I felt much better now that it was out. It didn't feel like stalking at the time, but looking back now, the truth of the matter was clear. I was a crazy girlfriend, and I was ashamed.

"Hey, it's OK; I was just worried for you. That's probably not the safest place for you to be alone."

Easton was understanding and forgiving.

"I just wanted to find you. I—"

"Shhh, it's fine." Easton ran his hand through my hair. "Did he say anything to you?" he asked.

"It was an . . . odd, exchange. He kind of acted like you were just a bar buddy and not his grandson. Now looking back . . ." I glanced up at Easton, and though I saw nothing, I stared, waiting for his answer.

"He knows me as a poker buddy. I know him as a little brother."

I sat straight up, "What!?" I wanted to search his eyes, but it was so dark that all I could see was a moonlit silhouette.

"Two lives ago, he was my little brother. When I moved out for college, he was seven. It was a bad home. An abusive one. It's always weighed on my heart. I shouldn't have left him there alone. But, it's not the first time I've seen it. Lived it. And it won't be the last. I spent my last life looking for him to no avail. I ended that one short. I was twenty years old when I gave up on that one."

Easton played with my locks, reflecting on his past life.

"I found Clyde at that bar, completely by chance. He didn't remember me, but I knew it was him. I made it my mission to get to know him and hopefully find a way to enrich his life. So far, I've only made him laugh. He's a tough nut to crack, and I think his substance abuse makes him damn near impenetrable. Still, I try."

"It makes so much sense now."

I laid my head back on Easton's shoulder and pondered the awkward conversation we had outside of the bar.

I began to chuckle. "I probably looked like such an idiot to him!"

Easton found amusement in this. "I'm sorry. Grandpa just seemed like the closest thing I could think of at the time to convey how much he meant to me."

I traced hearts over Easton's chest. The pad of my finger barely pressing into his T-shirt. I felt terrible for him. It made me think of ways to make him feel better.

"That reminds me. Guess who I ran into tonight?" I said.

"Who?" Easton's heart was beginning to pulse under my hand.

"Simon."

"You ran into Simon? Tonight?"

"Yeah," I began to chuckle again. I rolled over to grab my phone.

"I brought him to the karaoke bar with us, and we all sang on stage together! It was a riot!"

I pulled up the multiple selfies I took of Simon and me, Simon and the crazy one, Simon and the girl who was . . . still not Alice. I paged through the photos in the dark, and Easton squinted, as the light was bright in his eyes.

"I don't remember that girl's name, but she was nice. And that's when Simon and I took shots!"

Easton shot me a look I could only see by the light of my phone.

"What? I didn't drink that much; It was only like three or four drinks."

Easton continued to stare in disbelief.

I laughed, "I'm serious! I don't think my body can process liquor like it used to. I felt sick after just one drink! But, then I drank more to squash the social awkwardness. It's a real struggle sometimes."

Easton's disbelief turned humorous. His face cracked into laughter.

I laughed too, but I didn't know what we were laughing at, just that his mood was contagious. The more I laughed, the harder he did.

"Beck?" Easton managed to squeak as he wiped a tear from his eye.

I sat on the edge of the bed. My phone was still lighting up his glorious smile.

"Huh?" I giggled, half dazed, half confused.

"That's . . . *not* Simon!"

"What!"

I grabbed my phone from him and examined the photos. Easton was laughing so hard now he was rolled over to his side, his arm hanging off the bed. I shot to my feet and flipped on the overhead lights. I studied the selfies as if they would conjure an explanation.

They didn't.

I wanted to say something, but my jaw just hung open as I watched Easton roll around in hysteria. My face flushed; I wanted to get him. But all I could think of was the pillow. I grabbed a throw pillow from the floor and chucked it at his face. In a million years, I would never make that shot, but tonight, I did.

The pillow knocked the laughter right out of his mouth. Now he was as shocked as I was.

We stared at each other for a split second with pure animalistic instincts. Without a strategy, I picked up the second throw pillow, but I was too slow. The first of the ammunition was fired back and already hurtling toward my head. I turned as it slammed into my shoulder.

I screamed.

Easton flew out of bed, ready to attack; I screamed louder and tried to run away. He was impossibly quick. He grabbed me around the waist, and I laughed so hard that no sound escaped my throat.

Easton grunted, pinning me to the bed. I fought with as much strength as I had. It wasn't nearly enough to make a difference.

Both of us struggled to catch our breath. Our heart's throbbing against each other.

I broke out into laughter once again, but something in Easton's eyes melted my hysteria into depths of desire. The air shifted. For a moment, I took it in, the look in his eyes, the pounding of his chest. It was a moment I never wanted to forget.

"Do you," Easton began, breathless.

I rolled my bottom lip in between my teeth, trying to freeze time. I wished I could live in that instant forever, basking in the light of Easton's most cherished love.

I lifted my head, searching his eyes just long enough for my lips to find his. Time slipped away as we succumbed to our passion. It was the moment of a lifetime—the moment when I learned the difference between having sex and making love. I had never done the latter. It was the night I was able to convey just how much Easton meant to me. And I did so with every slide of my hand. Every plush kiss of my lips. The driving thrust of my hips. It was a slow, sultry dance to a melody only he and I could hear. The emotional bond we had, collided in a storm of lust and desire.

The sunlight penetrated my eyelids, and I scrunched my eyes while spreading my arms wide, stretching, and reaching. When I felt nothing but the cold sheets to my side, my eyes flung open, and I sat up.

I looked around my room for signs of Easton, but everything was unnervingly still. The dust sparkled in the air as it sank to the floor. In the distance, a car door slammed. My love, not lost. Not yet. I bolted to my bathroom and took a swig of mouthwash. My head pounding all the way. I perked up when I heard fumbling in my entryway. I spat and hurdled back into my bed, finding my warm spot. My anticipation grew with each footstep on the stairs.

"Hey, how are you feeling?" Easton asked, holding a tray of coffee and a bag of what I presumed to be pastries. I could get used to this. A flush of my cheeks was enough to answer his question—and more. A dimple kissed his cheek.

"I feel surprisingly light today." My eyes wandered the bedding. Easton laughed.

My heart began to pound. Maybe it was embarrassment, for the heat of passion last night was now out in the open daylight. Perhaps it was so surreal that I wanted to see if it would happen again.

My mouth watered as the nutty warmth of coffee wafted through the air. Easton closed the distance. He placed the coffee and the bag of treats down on my nightstand. Without a thought in my head, I reached out. Wrapping my finger into his belt loop, and I pulled him toward me.

Sometimes, it's luck. Sometimes the stars align so

perfectly, the unthinkable happens. Then, there are times where dreams meet reality. It boils down to fate. It didn't matter where my stars fell from here on out. I'd found Easton, and I wasn't going to let go—today, physically speaking. We'd spend the day fooling around in bed until the daylight gave way to the darkness. Beyond that, I don't know what it meant. But I'd have to imagine that when I passed on, my heart would be staying with him. Because I was no longer its owner.

CHAPTER 22

hloe's mom placed a delicate crystal tiara in her daughter's hair. It was the finishing touch to the most beautiful bride I'd ever seen. Even though she wasn't the bride I would have handpicked for my brother, she was the one that was meant to be. And that made her beautiful. Sometimes there are right choices and wrong choices. Sometimes it's right for *right now*. I had high hopes she would be my brother's *Harold*. And if I, for some reason, turned into a ghost after all of this was over, I would follow them and do what I could to keep them on track. Likewise, I might haunt her if she ever did him wrong.

It was probably my ignorance talking. Perhaps my love for my brother. But it was hard to imagine anyone having a bond like the one that I shared with Easton. I knew it was special. But I would even go as far as to say it was one-of-a-kind love. And if that was the case, where did that leave Carter and Chloe? Where did that leave all the other couples in the world? Was love on a spectrum?

"She looks stunning, doesn't she?" Mom whispered in my ear. She had tears in her eyes.

"Mom, you're going to ruin your makeup before the wedding even starts!" I shook my head. What was she doing? "Control yourself," I scolded with a half-smile, both appalled by and poking fun of her weakness.

She slapped my shoulder and dabbed the corners of her eyes with a tissue. "Stop that!" she hissed.

It was in those tears that I realized how difficult this evening would be for me. Because for every tear my mom would shed, I would have none. I couldn't find it in my heart to forget my unfortunate fate. Though, that's what I needed to do for the happiness to peek through. It's not the dying part that upset me, but all the things I'd never be able to do. All of the moments I'd miss out on. And on such a momentous night, I realized I was afraid to watch what I could never have.

My mom handed me a full glass of champagne. My stomach churned. I looked around the room at the women brought together as a mark of Chloe's past and future.

I was neither. Chloe's mother held her glass up, "To my little girl, my starlight, my Coco . . ."

I sighed. On accident.

"I'm so happy you've found your soulmate. To a life filled with happiness and babies! Lots and lots of babies!" Her mom held her champagne in the air and gave Chloe an air kiss on both cheeks. Her grandmother grumbled something inaudible as she lifted her glass before downing it in two gulps.

I didn't pretend. I just placed my champagne flute, as

full as it was given to me, on a table near my side. My mom set her empty glass on the table before picking up mine and swallowing it. She gave me a look, out of the corner of her eye, as she gulped it down. A look I didn't recognize and couldn't decipher.

I walked down the aisle on the arm of Carter's best friend Nick. His best man. Fresh daisies and red ribbon lined the church's pews and covered an arch above the minister's head. Guests filled the seats, and I could feel the stares. I was suddenly less focused on the irony of my childhood dream—walking down the aisle with my older brother's best friend—and more focused on not tripping. My heels were a good four inches, and that was about four inches more than I knew how to walk in. I never had the chance to practice, though I had planned to. Nick smiled and nodded at the strangers on each side of the aisle. He was a natural, and had my life taken another path, this could have been my reality. I looked down, not to see a white wedding gown but a thin satin shift dress. Purple.

I took my place on stage and stole a peek at Easton. He sat in the second row, wearing a black suit and a warm, encouraging smile. His hair was gelled so that it still looked disheveled, but in a way that would not come undone. I imagined him standing in the mirror, trying to get it just right. It was working to calm my nerves.

When the "Wedding March" began, and all invasive eyes turned to the back of the room, I took a deep sigh of relief. I looked down at my heels and took several therapeutic breaths. I didn't want to see the bride in all her glory. I was afraid of what I might feel. Jealousy was the green-eyed bitch, and I didn't need that weighing on my conscience. I looked to Easton instead. Our eyes met. A stolen moment in a room full of people. He gave me the courage to face my inner struggle. To face the bride as she walked down the aisle—a vision that is every little girl's dream.

It was as painful as I imagined. Chloe beamed with love from head to toe. Her normal tackiness subdued. And if I didn't know her, I might even say she looked elegant. Her hands were buried deep in daisies and a large red ribbon bow. Her tiara sparkled as much as her eyes as she set her sights on my brother. Carter's gaze met hers, and it wasn't until that moment, when I saw the joy emitting from my brother, that I realized I had room in my heart to be both happy for them and sad for me, all at the same time.

I threw my head back, willing the tears to suck back in their ducts, but it was no use. I was my mother's daughter. I gave up, lowered my head, and they ran freely down my cheeks. I glanced at Easton, who was now sympathetic. They must have been some tears if he could see them from the second row. I only hoped that waterproof mascara wasn't a gimmick.

If I thought I was losing it then, I was mistaken. My tears were just warming up. A mere appetizer to a five-course meal. The night was young, and the handwritten vows had yet to begin.

"Chloe, when you came into my life, I wasn't thinking of settling down and getting married. But when I got to know you, and I saw what you were doing to me, I knew that I would be stupid to let you go. You make me want to be a better person. And I promise you, from here on out, I will strive to be the best husband there ever was. And with you by my side, I think I can be that for you. I love you." Carter's vow was shaky and full of promise.

It's the second time in my life I'd seen my brother speak with such depth and emotion. The first being when Easton and I cornered him at his work to talk about his bride.

I didn't have a good view of Chloe's face, so I peered down into her bouquet of daisies in my hand when she spoke her vows.

"Carter, it's with—" Chloe cleared her throat and stiffened her notes in front of her, and began again.

"Carter, it is with you, that I have finally found myself. I know, when I look into your eyes, not only who I am, but who I want to be. Thank you for being the kind, loving, and accepting man that you are. And thank you for taking me on as your co-captain. It won't be easy; I can promise you that. But it will be a life to remember, full of love and laughter. I can't wait to see what our future holds with my hand in yours. I love you." Chloe choked. I lifted my eyes to see her folding up her notes into a tiny square.

My mind drifted to a faraway place; a place where it was me who was slipping into a wedding gown, and Easton waiting for me at the end of a long and lush rose covered aisle. The beautiful imagery in my head was shattered when the minister spoke.

"In sickness, and in health . . ."

My stomach cramped like a small dagger had been thrust into it. The rush of bitter acid in my throat. It was enough to make me cough. Tears welled up again, but this time for a different reason. My mouth was now sour, and I was relieved that soon, I would be able to get off the stage and out of the limelight. *Soon*, I promised myself.

"You may kiss the bride," the minister said.

My brother kissed his new bride, at first sweetly, then bending her over backward. Her leg kicked up in the air, and everyone cheered. My heart was so happy for him, but the smile never came. I hated myself for it. I felt like a burden. And if I could change anything about this whole process, I would change my control over how I acted. I wanted my genuine emotions to show. But it never came out that way. My happiness was shadowed by jealousy, and my fear was hidden in anger. My lack of control was clouded by sadness.

"You did great!" Easton reached for my arm. The masses were on their way out of the church. Some lingered behind to talk to friends or family.

"I cried," I informed him.

Easton smiled, "I know." I shot him a look of concern before he added, "but you can't tell!" in a rush of words, aimed to make me feel less self-conscious.

"I'm glad that's over. I felt like I might pass out, and there was this one point where I threw up in my mouth! Just a little." I pressed my hand to my forehead. All of the emotion was taking a physical toll on me.

"The hard part is over. Now let's have some fun." Easton grabbed me tight around the waist and pulled me into him. "Wow, this dress is thin!" His eyes widened and his grasp tightened.

"I know! I feel so naked!" I admitted.

Easton's hands wandered, stopping ever so slightly over my sacrum. "Are you . . ." His eyes glistened as his palm searched for a panty line.

I shook my head, trying to contain my embarrassment, though reveling in the fact that I could excite him so easily. "You dirty dog, is that all you think about?" I joked.

"Well, it's hard not to notice these little details about you." Easton squeezed my waist, and I squealed in response.

The room was nearly empty, and I was aware that we should be heading to the reception hall. It was only a ten-minute drive from the church, and I couldn't be late.

"I'd love to hide here with you, but I need to get to the reception," I said.

"I'll drive."

It was a beautiful day for a wedding. The sky was painted in orange and pink as the sun set for the night, tired after a day's hard work. Easton and I walked hand in hand to his car, and I stabled my wobbly balance with his strength.

The reception hall was grand and I was impressed that it felt intimate, given its size. The dim overhead lights gave way to the romantic fairy lights sprinkled throughout the tables and buffet. Candles glowed on every white tablecloth, and daisies were tucked in every nook and cranny. It was a lot of hard work that came together in the end in one beautiful display. My eyes wandered over the tables, and the guests finding their seats. I was sitting between Easton and Nick. If I had it my way, I wouldn't spend the night sandwiched between an old ember and a current flame. But, as I stated before, I was not in control of this beautiful disaster that was my life.

I took my seat, thankful for the reprieve. It had only been a handful of weeks since I was diagnosed, but I felt the toll beginning to take hold. The air had shifted ever so slightly, and I was starting to notice things. Little things. Like, I always felt like I was fighting off a cold. I had to take a three-hour nap mid-morning just to have the strength to socialize tonight. I imagined it must be how the elderly felt. Napping. Being exhausted from doing nothing more than watching their soap operas. It sounded quite nice, actually. Tranquil almost.

I noticed my voice cracking more often too. Now and then, it would feel like something was lodged in my throat. A pill capsized halfway down. My breathing had been reduced to sucking air through a straw. The moment I noticed that the symptoms were too apparent to ignore, I began to hide them. Much like I did with my doctor's missed telephone calls, I tried to sweep my destiny under the rug. Out of sight, out of mind. But I knew it didn't work this way, and I knew at some point—hopefully, later than sooner—they would not go unnoticed. It was then, and only then when I would succumb to telling my parents.

CHAPTER 23

Nick took his seat next to me but not before he held a chair out for his date. She was a pretty, blond-haired girl, and if I wasn't mistaken, I thought she looked a lot like me. But unlike me, she wore a dress that was both sexy and obscure.

"Hey, Beckette, you did great out there!"

Nick called me by an old familiar nickname. He called my brother Beck, and even though my friends called me the same, he had to have a way to differentiate between the two of us. Hence, Beckette.

"That was nerve-wracking, huh? All of those eyes!" I turned my attention to his girlfriend. "Hi, I'm Carter's sister, Everly."

I reached over Nick and shook her hand. Ugh . . . it was a limp one. Before I could introduce Easton, Nick had done it himself, leaning into me as he shook Easton's hand. The whole exchange more like a game of Twister than anything else.

I felt the subtlety of his lean into my chest. Not noticeable to either of our dates, but a closeness deemed unnecessary. It seems that I may not have been the only one with revived memories of our youth dredging up old feelings by walking down the aisle together.

I reached my hand over the back of Easton and rubbed his shoulder. A public display of affection. Nick responded with a mirrored image as he claimed his date. The small talk began. Nick sized up Easton, asking what he did for a living and yada, yada, yada. I once valued this information myself. Not because of how fat his wallet was with potential but because of the insight of interests and drive. Now I only cared what Easton's soul looked like. Not his face or body. I didn't care what he did for work or fun. One hundred percent of my love for him was based on something intangible and something you could never uncover with a question from across the dinner table.

Our last couple joined us at the table, completing our setting for six. It was Alice and her date. A cute nerdy boy with box-rimmed glasses and suspenders.

"Hi everyone. Hi Everly!" Alice waived to me.

I smiled, thankful to have someone I liked at our table.

"I'm Audrey, and this is Benjamin."

Audrey!

My heart skipped a beat at the thought that I almost introduced her to our table under the wrong name . . .

"Oh! I've heard so much about you and all the fun you had with . . ."—Easton looked at me, eyes filled with mischief—"Simon!"

I thrust my jaw to the side and gave his shoulder a squeeze that was more like a pinch. *He wouldn't!*

Audrey threw her freckled face back and cackled like a witch. "Oh, your girl Everly's a riot!"

"Ohhh, you have no idea!" Easton's eyes beamed.

I stiffened at his side. My face flushed red with the embarrassment of spending an entire evening with a man I thought was someone else. The only thing more embarrassing than that would be if Easton told the story right here, right now. The butterflies swirled in my chest at the very thought.

I was lucky enough to be reminded why I loved him so much; he kept my secret a joke between the two of us, right where it belonged. But the embarrassment of that night wasn't all under lock and key. Audrey had memories of her own to spill, and that she did. The table laughed along with her as she retold her version of the night. I laughed at the fact that the truth was far more outrageous. And she would never know.

Everyone stood with applause when the bride and groom were announced. Waiters and waitresses swarmed the room, spreading salad plates and pouring either red or white wine. I chose red, even though I wouldn't take more than a taste. My hot plate of chicken breast, asparagus, and garlic roasted potatoes looked as divine as it smelled, but it wasn't enough to bring back my appetite. I spent a long time moving the food around on my plate so that I would look at least half engaged, but the truth was, my stomach had turned sour during the ceremony, and it had yet to recover.

"How do you all know the bride and groom?" Benjamin gestured to the rest of the table guests with his fork.

I took a deep breath, preparing myself for an answer, but Nick beat me to it.

"I've grown up with the Becks. Carter and I go way back! Everly too." Nick put his elbow in my side.

"Yeah, it was Nick, my brother, and Hope. A couple other kids that I didn't know very well too, but we all lived in the same neighborhood and grew up together. There was always a plethora of neighborhood kids at one house or another at any given time," I added.

Nick knew that I never hung out with them. Nobody wants to hang out with their little sister, anyway. His angle made me nervous, and I wondered if he was trying to intimidate Easton. The joke was on him, though; that would never work.

"How did you two meet?" Nick's girlfriend asked Audrey.

"Oh, we met in middle school, but we didn't start dating until after high school graduation." Audrey shook her head as if there was no story there. "What about you guys, Everly? How did you meet?" Audrey threw the ball in my court.

A panic set over me. I wasn't as rehearsed as Easton was. "Oh!" I scrambled to remember the story he told my parents about the bridge. He'd altered it so that I had a flat tire.

"We met at a college party!" Easton said as he stretched tall and placed his arm around my shoulders. "Craziest night of my *life!*"

This ought to be good . . . I couldn't keep my smile in. I was embarrassed about the lie yet excited to hear the make-believe memory. It was a new identity. And if I could be someone else just for that moment, I was going to do it.

"I saw her there." Easton placed a hand out like he was remembering me, and I snickered, covering my mouth with my hands. "She was like an angel. I fell for her without ever knowing her name. She looked at me from across the room, and we just knew." Easton's voice trailed off as he shook his head back and forth for dramatic flair.

I was sucked into the story as was the rest of the table. Only Nick stirred with disinterest.

"The cops rushed in, and everybody fled each and every way. But my eyes were set on Everly. I made sure that where she ran, I followed. We darted out of the house and down the streets. The crowd dwindled to half a dozen of us. It was someone's bright idea to take refuge in his friend's house that was only a couple of blocks away. But his friend wasn't home! What were we to do now?"

I bit my bottom lip and watched Easton capture the attention of the table.

"He started to check the windows! He said that his friend always left one open. And there it was, a window in the back of the house, unlocked. We took turns crawling through the window. We turn on the lights, start making quesadillas. Not long after that, the cops burst into that house as well! One went out the window, one got caught, two fled through the slider door, and Everly and I . . . we hid in the pantry!"

I burst into laughter. The others were on the edge of their seat. I watched Easton wrap up an epic story.

"Nine hours! Nine hours, was how long we had to hide until the homeowners left the house, and we could sneak out. It was the best damn nine hours of my life! And we've been together ever since."

The girls swooned, myself included. Even Benjamin thought it was an impressive love story.

"I thought it was his friend's house!" Audrey choked out.

Easton shook his head, "In his drunken state, he miscalculated by two doors down! Turns out it was an old retired English professor's house. Mr. Rottermen."

Audrey wailed, and I gave Easton a kiss on the cheek. And for a split second, I forgot that it was merely make-believe.

The bride and groom were called to the dance floor, and we watched as they shared their first dance. Carter was uncomfortable, no doubt, but he hid it well. The moment Chloe's father stepped in to have the father-daughter dance is the moment I felt my throat close. My eyes no longer able to watch; I dismissed myself to use the restroom. All the while, I thought about how I would never have the chance to dance with my pops at my wedding.

I stood in the bathroom much longer than necessary. If I were hiding from my emotions, it was a poor hiding place. I ran my hands under the cold water until they felt like ice. Then I placed them on my cheeks and the back of my neck. I was tired already, but I had a little while longer to last.

By the time I resurfaced, the heartfelt scene had

dissipated, and the party had started. Drinks were flowing, and the dance floor was on fire. I was thankful that it would be all downhill from here. There was still the cake to cut, but I didn't see how that could make me sad. Maybe I would be sad if my appetite hadn't yet returned, but that was one thing that I was confident I could handle.

I took my seat next to Easton. Our chairs were now turned to watch the dance floor. I loved to watch people dance. Some didn't care, some were gifted, others nervous and awkward. My favorite was when there was a combination of the ones who didn't care and the ones who were incredibly inept. They made for the best entertainment. I'd once seen a guy run and dive onto the varnished dance flooring, sliding like a penguin on his belly. He took out three people ending in a small dog pile in the middle of the crowd.

I was so content I didn't notice Nick when he approached us.

"Dance with me!" He held his hand out in front of me, vodka permeated the air.

"Oh, no, I couldn't." I shook my head and looked at Easton. Not for permission, but for rescuing. He smiled, not an ounce of jealousy in his eyes. If anything, maybe there was some sympathy. Not for me but Nick. Easton knew he would never have a chance.

I rolled my eyes, now feeling sorry for the sucker myself. I placed my hand in Nick's as I glared at Easton. He laughed and waved me farewell. The dance Nick and I shared was that of me taking a step back and him following. Him wrapping his hand around my waist, and me twisting out of it. It didn't take long for Easton to see that it was no longer fun and games. He stood to attention and made his way over after reading my several glaring attempts to call for help. Nick was harmless, but I didn't want someone's paws all over me. Especially not in this dress. Just before Easton approached us, the song turned to a slow romantic number. Nick caressed my back one last time before Easton tapped him on the shoulder.

"Mind if I cut in? This is our song," Easton lied.

He didn't wait for Nick's sloppy rebuttal. In one swift motion, I was secured in Easton's arms where I belonged.

I laid my head on his chest and sighed in relief. "Thank you."

"How are you holding up?" he asked.

I closed my eyes for a moment and then let it all fall out.

"Honestly? It's been a ride. I keep thinking about how I'll never have these memories of my own. It's hard to watch my parents." I looked up at Easton. "There's just so much I want to do, and there's not enough time." I searched the depth of his blue eyes, but it was dark, and I couldn't find my way into them.

Easton stopped our slow momentum.

"Marry me," he said.

My heart skipped a beat. Did I hear him correctly? I scanned his eyes more frantically now.

"Marry me!" he said again.

CHAPTER 24

"Marry you?" I repeated.

It took me a long while to process his request. I'd all but forgotten we were in the middle of a dancefloor. Time stood still.

"Why would you want to do that to yourself? I mean, it's one thing to have love and loss, but it's another to be a widower your whole life. Surely you don't want that title. And for what? I'll love you just the same . . ."

"I want to marry you! I'm not going to be a widower . . ."

Easton grabbed my elbow and led me to a more private place to continue our conversation without others overhearing. There, out in the hall, he said it. The thing I never considered. The thing that made me hate and love all the same.

"I'm not going to let you die alone!" Easton's forehead lined with pain.

His words like a dagger to my chest. I wouldn't have the

man I love die on my behalf. Even if he would resurrect sometime later or believe that he would.

"No! Are you crazy!? You can't do that!" I hissed. Eyes darting down the length of the hall. Still, no one within earshot.

"Everly, I don't think you understand! I've died a handful of times over, and I'll be damned if I let you do it alone!"

My skin began to heat. It's all I remember until I woke in Easton's lap with a small crowd hovering over me. Regrettably, one of them was a paramedic.

"What's happening?" I asked Easton in a storm of confusion and faintness.

"Shhh. Everything's OK. You've just been out for a little while," Easton said.

I looked at the paramedic; it must have been longer than a little while. The questions began to fire, but I couldn't answer any of them truthfully. None could be said in front of my mother, who was standing behind Easton.

"We should take her in, run some tests," the paramedic said to my mom.

My protest went unheard. Neither Easton nor I had a say in the matter, and before I knew it, I was placed on a gurney and rolled out of the reception hall. I convinced my mom that Carter would never forgive her if she left his wedding early and that Easton was more than capable of going with me to the hospital.

My mom watched me from the curb as they closed the ambulance doors. I was utterly mortified by my grand exit. And I'd thought the purple dress was bad.

"Is it Tim?" I asked the paramedic as I tried to focus my eyes on his name tag.

"Yes, it is."

"My boyfriend asked me to marry him, so I passed out," I mumbled.

Maybe it was the needle in my arm, or maybe it was Tim's kind face, but truth poured out of me now that my mom was out of sight.

Tim chuckled. "Is that the boy who's following us in that beamer?"

"Yes."

"You did all that to get out of saying, no?" Tim asked.

"No! I wanted to say yes . . . but here's the kicker: I have cancer." I rubbed my throat as I said it. "Have you heard of anaplastic thyroid cancer?" I asked.

Tim's face contorted with sympathy. He'd heard of it. Less than one percent of thyroid cancer mutates into such a demon.

"It's spread, and I don't have long."

"Why didn't you tell me this back at the wedding, dear?" Tim asked.

"I haven't told my parents," I admitted. It would be the most expensive therapy session I'd ever receive.

Tim sighed and ran his eyes through the cab before returning to me. "And what about the boy?"

"He's the only one that knows. I told him the night we met."

I thought back to it, surprised by my behavior. It was then when I realized I never actually told him. I wouldn't have. Not even in a fury of panic.

"Are you afraid to marry the boy because of what it will do to him when you're gone?" Tim asked as he checked my vitals.

"Something like that," I mused.

"Well, dear, I don't have an answer for you. But if the boy asked, and he knows, I'm guessing he's already made his decision." Tim had no idea how profound his simple comment was.

He was right. Easton had already made his decision. He was going when I was. Regardless if we'd end up in the same place or not. It wouldn't stop him from trying. I couldn't control Easton's life any more than I could control mine.

I ran through the gauntlet of tests, and Easton waited patiently. And when the doctor came in to tell me my latest updates, he was there by my side. The cancer was in my thyroid, trachea, lymph nodes, and now my liver. It would soon spread to my lungs and bones. It wasn't news to me, but hearing it out loud was a different kind of pain. The kind that made your face wince and your body squirm. The hours ticked by, and the sky had begun to lighten by the time I was discharged. I would later tell my mom it was dehydration.

That was, until I found the right moment for the truth that would shatter her heart. Was there ever a fitting moment for such a thing? The burden was now too heavy to carry on my own. I needed to admit it to myself and everyone I loved that I needed help. I could see now from this event that it was unfair of me to place such a heavy burden on Easton alone.

"Easton?" I asked, looking out his car window.

"Huh?"

"I don't believe I ever told you I had cancer." I turned my attention to his face. "How did you know?" I studied him. He glanced up into his rearview mirror, then to me.

"I *know* things. I can't explain it."

"Try." I was short.

"The same way I can tell if another is a Tethered Soul, I feel it. Their spirit's age, fine like wine. Perfected as much as a flawed being can be. I feel their pain—too grand for one life alone."

Easton glanced over to see how I was taking the news, then he studied the road ahead of him. "It's the same as when I met you. I knew when you pulled me off of the bridge . . . the very instant when I looked into your eyes on the sidewalk. Your heart was meant for me. A perfect soulmate in an imperfect world. But I felt your time was limited, like a battery draining low. I would live forever, and you would perish shortly thereafter meeting you. The only thing worse was the thought of never knowing you at all."

Easton spoke quietly, his words laced with the heartache only he could ever know.

"Yes," I whispered. The word spilled out onto my breath.

Easton's brows furrowed as his eyes shifted between me and the road.

"Yes," I said. My voice raspy, but I meant it with all that I was.

"I want to marry you! I want to spend the rest of my life loving you. I don't have much to give, but—"

"Beck, don't. Let me be the judge of that." Easton reached over and squeezed my hand. His eyes were wet with love.

CHAPTER 25

t was just dehydration! . . . Yeah, they gave me an IV, and I went home."

I paced around my living room, watching my feet as they continued their shuffle. It was the moment I lifted my gaze and caught Easton's expression that I knew I was doing more harm than good. I listened to my mom on the other line. Then, with a heavy heart, I asked.

"Mom? Can I come by today?"

The minutes began to tick as soon as I got off the phone. Ninety short minutes was all I had to prepare myself to tell my parents that they would be alive to bury their daughter. I grabbed at my stomach when it churned with nausea and sat down on the sofa. Still exhausted from the night spent in the hospital, the climb I had ahead of me seemed damn near impossible.

Easton rubbed my shoulders and kissed the top of my head. I looked up at him, suddenly upset that I had made this decision, here and now.

"Don't make me do this alone!"

"Never. I'll be right by your side," he said.

"Hi, honey! Come on in!" My mom kissed my cheek and pulled me inside. "Thanks for taking care of her, Easton!" Mom kissed his cheek, too.

We stepped into the shadows of the house. My eyes took longer than usual to adjust. Dad was watching a game on TV and said hello with a wave from the couch. My first concern was getting him to turn the TV off. Sure, it was as simple as asking, but I'd never asked my parents to stop what they were doing and give me their full attention. I didn't want to worry them. And yet, that's what I had come here to do. I dispelled the thought with a shake of the head. It had to be said. I believed that now.

"Can I get you two an iced tea? You have to stay hydrated!" Mom said. I wished it was that simple.

"Yeah, that sounds great, Mom."

I moved to the sofa and joined my dad. He gave me a pat on the knee. The secret that I'd been holding in since early March was growing heavier. It came out by way of clammy palms and ringing ears. My legs began to tremble.

"Well, you didn't miss much last night. After you left, everything kind of just wound down. We threw rice at your brother and his wife. Oh! I get to say that now! His *wife*!" Mom said.

Two ice teas were set in front of Easton and me. He took a polite sip, but I was too nervous to move.

"I'm so glad you two are paying us some attention! I know you're so busy with work and school—it's like I never get to see you anymore!" Mom said. More bricks added to my already too heavy load.

"I quit my job!" I blurted out. It was the first of many to come. Dad flinched but continued watching the game.

"Oh, well . . . if you need help with the bills, I'm sure we could—"

"I stopped going to school, too. So . . . maybe you should stop paying for my tuition."

That got my dad's attention. He reached for the remote and turned the TV off. Nobody said anything. The tension boiled inside me like a pressure cooker. I rubbed my wet hands onto my jeans. I wanted to say it in a way that wouldn't hurt, but I feared it would tumble out just like my other confessions and catch fire.

My mom cleared her throat, unable to say anything nice. She held it in and waited for my dad to speak.

"You kids these days think that a college education isn't worth squat, but—"

"There's more, Dad. Dad?" He continued to talk over me. Ramblings of the value I couldn't see.

"Dad!" I yelled.

The mood shifted. What once was disappointment was now shock. Soon, it would be devastation. I should have rehearsed it. Came up with the perfect way to tell them. But I didn't, and they were going to have to live with my mistake.

"I . . . didn't pass out because I was dehydrated. I passed out because I'm fighting . . . um, an illness. And my immune system is working really hard, but it can't do it all," I said.

I refused to look at them, but I could feel the disarray pass through the thick air.

"What? Like cancer?" Dad asked.

"No! Don't say that!" hissed my mom.

"Yes," I replied.

Mom sucked in a sharp breath. I kept my eyes glued to the floor. A shower of shame rained down upon me. As if it were my doing, my choice.

"Well, we're going to fight it! I'm going to call Doctor Allen. He'll know what to do!"

Mom jumped to her feet. She walked herself in a couple of circles before making it to the phone. Fight or flight was a common reaction. Like my mom, the fight was my first response too. Until the doctor showed me the images. My chance to fight was fleeting.

Arguing erupted overhead as Pops tried to change her course of action. Shots fired back and forth, fueled by fear. I sat silenced. My knuckles, white. When Easton reached his limit, he stood and began to speak of the facts. And just as he did, my parents shifted their focus to learning what they could instead of changing what they'd yet to understand.

"Everly had papillary thyroid cancer. The symptoms were easy to overlook, and she was young. She had a biopsy done via fine-needle aspiration. That's when a tiny needle goes into the nodule and collects cells. Unfortunately, the specific cells collected in this fine needle tip were not the cells that were mutated, but the surrounding cells from her thyroid. Her results were inconclusive. It's a usual reading. More times than not, it means there's no cancer."

Easton commanded the room much like he did when he told the make-believe story of how we met at my brother's wedding. I assumed that he had gathered all of this information after he read my medical files in the hospital. Perhaps he'd spoken to my doctor. The air was so thick that I was sure I would suffocate right then and there, never making it my full term. My parents were frozen. It was the most I'd ever seen them focus on anything in my entire life. They absorbed every morsel of detail that Easton spilled, while I sat on the couch dripping with guilt, sweat, and tears.

"On rare occasions—less than one percent—thyroid cancer will morph. The cells will mutate into a highly abnormal and aggressive form of cancer called anaplastic. The prognosis is poor. And in Everly's case, it has already spread. I regret to inform you that she is not a candidate for chemotherapy and radiation. Her cancer is resistant to treatment." Easton spoke with poise. His performance was captivating.

Darkness blanketed the sky as it did the hearts of my parents. It took a long time to convince them this was their new reality. What felt like an eternity, was probably closer to a couple of hours. But they were some of the most challenging hours of my twenty-two years. There had been breakdowns, and several stages of acceptance. Shock, anger, denial, and bargaining. I knew that they would continue to play on repeat for quite some time, but I held on to the hope that eventually, they would cycle out of these stages and move through depression and finally, one day, acceptance. Possibly, they could find happiness there.

Mom was stuck in denial. She was racking her brain over all the possibilities. As if I hadn't already considered all of it.

"Mom, stop! I'm exhausted! I've already accepted that I'm on the fast track. I'm not saying you must also, but you need to respect my decision during this time. I'm not a kid anymore! I'm the mature woman that you raised me to be, and this is my life. And I've chosen not to spend the rest of it in the hospital or hovering over the toilet, sick. I don't want an experimental treatment! I don't! There's nothing they can do anyway. And I'm OK with it. I'm focusing on my quality of life now. And Easton's been helping with that. We've been experiencing things I've always dreamed of. It's been some of the best weeks of my life, and I mean that!"

Mom's face melted into her hands, and she began to weep again. Pop helped to hold her as her knees buckled. It was hard to witness and even worse to know I was the cause of it.

"I'm sorry I didn't tell you sooner. I wish I'd been stronger. I wasn't. I was afraid of hurting you guys."

Despite how much I cared for them, I just wanted it to be over. I willed them to see it from my perspective—to give me the green light that I needed to live my life as I saw fit. I pushed off the couch and walked to the fireplace. Had there been a fire going, my arm wouldn't have been so cold pushed against the red brick. Easton was getting antsy too. He'd moved to the kitchen to get some water.

"Look, I don't know what's going to happen when I die, but if for some reason I'm still here on earth, following you two around, I'm going to be really pissed if you guys are sad all the time. I just want you to be happy when you think of me. I want to be celebrated. I want to feel the love, not the sorrow!" I ran my fingers through my hair as I felt the last remaining fight drain out of me. "Would it be too much to ask for that while I'm alive too?" I searched the eyes of my mom, then my dad. Both sets were red and swollen.

After a long moment of unspoken despair, my dad pulled me into his embrace. Everyone was out of things to say and had all but given up. I pressed my ear against his heart and took comfort in its beat and the smell of vanilla tobacco.

"There's one more thing," I said.

Pops groaned. He couldn't bear any more news. I looked to Easton, and for the first time that day, I felt a shift in my mood. I buried my face into my dad's chest and squinted my burning eyes tight for a moment before pulling away.

"We're getting married . . ."

Easton's face lit with pride as he thrust to his feet and re-entered the room, ready for hugs. My parents were a little slower to react.

My eyes flickered between the three pairs of eyes. Two uncertain, and one losing hope. Did I need to explain myself? Wasn't it obvious? Had we not gone through this for the last two or three hours? "Pop! I love him! And I'm going to spend the rest of my life with him! Now, I would appreciate it if you celebrate our love and give me this last memory!" I said with a hand on my hip.

Like clockwork, my mom raised her arms to Easton, pulling him into an embrace and welcoming him to the family. It took a little coaxing, but it's what I wanted to see. A genuine smile spread across my face and into my eyes. My dad cried.

Regardless of the pain, heartbreak, and sheer exhaustion, I walked out of that dark house feeling lighter than I had in a long time. I felt the gravitational pull that tethered me to earth, to my body . . . disconnect. My spirit was beginning to free. I was halfway packed for my departure, and I wondered if this was a mandatory step in me letting go. As Easton opened my car door for me and I caught his eye, I realized something else.

The second half to cutting my tether was saying goodbye to Easton.

CHAPTER 26

It was well after dinner by the time that Easton took me home. He stayed to feed Yeti and made a small batch of pasta for the dinner that we'd missed. I didn't eat.

"Thank you. I couldn't have done it without you," I said. A plaid throw blanket wrapped around my shoulders.

Easton ate his dinner, leaning against the refrigerator. "I was happy to be there for you. It's never an easy conversation to have."

"You act like you've had it before. And how did you know all that stuff? I didn't even know all of it!" I said.

"I used to be a doctor. I glanced at your chart when you were resting at the hospital."

A doctor?

Why did this surprise me? I pictured Easton back in my parent's living room, breaking the news to them. It seemed as if he'd done it a hundred times before. And if I stretched my imagination just a little further and pictured him with a white coat, holding a clipboard, it almost made sense. My eyes began to blur as visions of my blue-eyed boyfriend became a doctor, and I knew it was time for me to go to bed. My mind was cooked, my heart hurt, and my eyes were playing tricks on me.

Easton stayed with me as he had been doing more often. I slept better with him here. Sometimes in the middle of the night, I would slide my foot over until I found his warmth. It was enough to soothe my anxiety and put me back to sleep. Other times, I would go overboard and wake up smothering him. But tonight, I did neither. Tonight, I slept like I was already six feet deep.

When the morning came, so did my mom. Easton let her in while I was still dead to the world. I woke up to the chatter downstairs. I slipped on a robe and headed down the stairs to see her, only stopping halfway when I heard her soft-spoken voice.

"Then you can text me when you're on your way. It's going to be her brother and his wife, her friends, Lindsay, Lisa, Shannon—"

The stairs creaked under my weight. I made myself known.

"Mom? What are you doing here?"

"I, um, well I wanted to see you. I know that last night was difficult. I brought you coffee and flowers."

Mom stood grasping a coffee from Fresh Grounds. The

bags under her eyes were as dark as her eyebrows, and she was still dressed in the same clothes from yesterday.

I took the coffee from her and wrapped my arms around her. Only then did I see Easton was sitting at the kitchen island in his boxers. He took the moment of my embrace and scurried upstairs. Presumably to get dressed, but maybe to give us privacy as well.

"Mom, I'm worried about you."

"No, you listen to me," Mom said. She sat me down at the island where Easton and she had shared a secret conversation just moments before. "I know I look like *trash*, but that's only because I stayed up all night . . ."

I raised my hand and slapped it down on my leg.

"I had a lot to think about. Now, I'm not saying I'm OK with this, but your dad and I talked, and we've come to the conclusion that you have enough on your plate. And the last thing you need is to be worried about us. We want your days filled with love and laughter. And, honey"—her eyes began to water, and her voice rose—"I promise you that I'm going to try my hardest to stay that way after too. And I hope that it can put your mind to ease."

Her chin wobbled as large tears ran down her cheeks. She crumbled into my chest. I wrapped my arms around my mom and held her as she wept. Tears streamed down my face as I stared out my window with blurry vision. Yeti's instincts took over and she nestled my mom, helping to break her episode.

"I know it's hard, Mom, but that's what I want. Thank you."

We shared our coffee talking about the wedding. I told

her how I envisioned it. No minister, no music, no audience, just Easton and I professing our love for one another and committing to the short time I had left. I was tired as it was, and I didn't want to have to entertain guests. In addition to that, I didn't want to say goodbye to all of them. It was hard enough to tell my parents. Extending that conversation to aunts and uncles, friends and co-workers . . . *no thank you*.

A wedding was about devoting your love to someone, and that's all I wanted from it. And maybe a ring. Nothing fancy. It could be made of twine or the stem of a daisy—just something to slip onto my finger.

It wasn't easy to convince my mom that a wedding could be anything other than traditional, but after a squeeze of her hand and a flash of pleading in my eyes, she stopped to listen.

My mom visited every day after that. Mostly, she would come mid-day as not to barge in before Easton had a chance to get dressed. Sometimes, my dad would accompany her. I would gush to her about Easton, and she would cry every time. But she was sleeping and changing her clothes, so things were looking up. Both of my parents were run down, but they tried their hardest to stay positive for me. Even though I could see through their charades, I appreciated the effort.

I was thankful that my parents did the heavy lifting when it came to Carter. They told him in private so that I wouldn't have to do it myself. When he had time to collect himself, he came over to see me. Chloe stayed back, but she baked homemade cookies and sent them with Carter. I knew she wanted to give us privacy to talk, and I respected that. But Carter and I didn't talk much. It wasn't his language. It wasn't that he didn't care—just that he didn't express himself with words. I still felt all of his emotion as we sat together in my living room. And I felt his body trembling when he hugged me goodbye. We all express ourselves in different ways, and a part of me took to the way Carter did it.

In the following days, I showed my mom where my letters were. We both cried over that one. And I told her all of the things Yeti liked and didn't like. I told her I wanted to be cremated.

There were few possessions I held dear to my heart, but I made a list of things that I felt were essential and I wanted my parents to disperse to loved ones. The rest, I wanted them to donate. And soon too. I saw no purpose for them to store boxes of my things in their garage for years to come. It wouldn't lessen the pain, and it wouldn't bring me back. My "keep list" contained only three things.

The first thing I cherished most in this world was a pair of diamond earrings my grandmother had given me when I graduated high school. She'd gotten them as a Mother's Day gift from her late son. The uncle I'd never met. Because she cherished them, I was nothing short of honored to have received them. I treated them as such too. I pulled them out of the top drawer of my dresser, where they'd been resting in a felt bag.

"Grandma gave me these."

My mom knew very well what they were. Her mother

wore them every day for two decades. That was, until she gifted them to me.

My mom sat quietly on my bed, reminiscing over the earrings and the very situation we found ourselves in.

"Actually, I'm going to wear these for the ceremony," I said.

It was funny how I saved them for a special occasion only. I never thought there would be a shortage of time or special occasions for me to wear them. If I had, I would have worn them every day as my grandmother did. It was a foolish way of thinking. And If I had it to do all over again, I would enjoy the things I loved most. I would wear them out until they were unusable, and then I would love them some more.

Instead of placing the earrings back in the drawer, I slipped them into my ears. My mom jumped up to help me with the backings. When she pulled away, tears had formed in her eyes. It wasn't often that I saw her without them.

The second tangible item I loved too much to see thrown out was my first stuffed animal. It was a tattered old frog that my mom got me when I was in utero. She thought I was a boy. It was a dream she had of two boys playing outside by a pond—fishing for crawdads. It could have been a premonition, in fairness to her, because my brother and I did go on to do that. And I could have passed as a boy with a baseball cap and a mud-painted face. Either way, I loved the frog. And I always imagined that I would give it to my firstborn.

"Can you give this to Carter's baby? When he has one."

I shrugged. "Maybe you could tell him it's from his Aunt Everly."

Carter's kids would be cuties. They would have his light complexion and Chloe's great bone structure. They would be loud and outspoken until it came time to express their emotions. They would have my green eyes.

My mom took the frog and cradled it in her lap. She forced a smile and waited patiently for me to continue.

"And, last but not least, these." I resurfaced from my closet, holding three diaries—one purple suede, one zebra print, and one, a more mature faux leather. Each resembled the maturity at which I started the journal.

I sat down on the bed next to my mom, and a picture fell out of the first book I opened. One of Lindsay and I in the sixth grade. Fake blood ran down our mouths and covered our hands. I remembered that day like yesterday.

"That was Halloween. She had the capsules of fake blood that you pop in your mouth," I said. I could still remember the way they tasted—like cough syrup.

I flipped through the zebra print diary. Pictures were glued to the pages, and a colorful display of rainbow ink bled across the pages. I ran my fingers over the imprinted pen marks. The more emotion poured onto the page, the more the words felt like reversed brail.

"What's that?" Mom pointed to a receipt I had taped into the journal.

"Huh. That was a receipt for a movie."

I glanced over the entry and read a quick blurb about how the love of my life sat behind me and threw popcorn at me during the movie. I was sure that he was the one. But I was eleven, and he was nothing more than a cute stranger.

I closed the journal, embarrassed by what was inside.

"On second thought, maybe we burn them?"

Mom laughed. She took the journals from my lap and added them to her collection of strange things that I deemed essential.

"I would never do that! I can't wait to read them. I'm allowed to read them, right?" she asked.

Should I let her read them? All I knew was that I cherished them. My memories and personal thoughts captured in three books. I wasn't sure that they should be *read*. What if it hurt her feelings? The last thing I wanted was to leave her with lasting anger from when I hit puberty!

My face contorted in regret. "No, seriously . . . let's burn them!"

"What! No! We can't do that!"

"Mom, I can't have you read all the times I was mad at you and took it out on my diary! That's cruel and unusual punishment!"

Mom's face twisted with the realization that there were in fact, negative things hidden deep within the pages.

"I won't read them, then. I'll wrap a bow around them and place them on my nightstand. I'll keep them close, but I won't read them."

I searched my mom's eyes. She was unwilling to let them go up in flames and smoke. Something so important to me couldn't be lost in such a way. I gave in.

"Tie it *tight*," I said.

CHAPTER 27

$\mathcal{M}$usic filled the air, and my mom twirled with a glass of wine in her hand. It was mid-day, and I happen to know she skipped breakfast. I only cared that she was happy, and it appeared that she was. She set her glass down, humming to the music, and separated a lock of my hair to be curled.

I watched myself in the mirror. I wasn't sure if my bathroom lights were washing my already pale complexion out, or if I was losing what little color I had, but my face was lackluster and sallow. It wasn't the familiar face of a glowing bride.

"Now, do you want it up, or maybe like this? Oh! This is romantic . . ." She held a single strand from the front and pinned it back behind my ear.

"Yeah, I like that."

"It's going to be cold, you know. A storm is coming in. You're going to need to wear a jacket. Even if it doesn't match your dress!" Mom said.

"I know."

I couldn't help but wonder what the girl in the mirror would look like a couple of years older and healthier. Mom finished my hair, placing a crystal pin in my trestle. She was right; it was romantic.

I stepped into my dress, holding on to my mom's arm for balance. While the dress was white, it was anything but traditional. More of a sundress than anything else. Woven eyelet flowers and lace. The straps were thin and crossed in the back. The length hit just above the knee but it had a generous and even sexy slit up one leg. It wouldn't show unless I took a step. Or perhaps twirled.

"You look gorgeous!" Mom clapped her hands to her mouth.

"Mom, stop! I look like I'm going to a backyard barbecue!" I tried to downplay the moment. But the truth was, I felt pretty special, and I was fighting back the tears myself.

"Can you put a little makeup on me?" I asked.

Though I never wore very much makeup myself, it wasn't because I didn't like it. I just preferred the natural look. Today, though, the natural look was unsettling. It had been growing worse as time slipped by. My mom dusted a muted mauve over my cheeks, bringing them back to life. A light highlight almost made me look lit from within. If I didn't know any better, I would say I looked almost thriving in a youthful, healthy way.

"Thank you, Mom," I said.

"Oh, honey. Thank you for letting me be a part of your special day. I wish I was there to see you."

"There's nothing to see. We're just spending time together. It's . . . I don't know . . . personal. It's only fitting to keep it private."

Our wedding was going to be as unique as our situation. One dying girl, and one undying boy. A love that would last forever. It wasn't for prying eyes. Only for the two of us to share with one another.

"Hello?" Easton called out from downstairs.

"Looks like it's that time!" I said to my mom. "Are you sure you can drive home?"

"Oh yeah. I've only had one glass!" Mom walked beside me as I went down the stairs, supporting my elbow even though I was barefoot and arguably more stable than she was.

Easton clasped his heart at first sight of me in my sundress.

"I'm honored. What did I do to deserve you?" Easton muttered as his eyes took in the length of me.

"Oh, I have to take a picture!" Mom waved her hands wildly and pranced over to her purse to retrieve her phone. I rolled my eyes. Though I completely understood and wanted a picture myself, I still hated to stand for the barrage of photos. It took away from the magic of the moment.

Easton wrapped his warm arms around my waist, and my mom snapped several photos as he kissed my temple and beamed with pride. I ignored my mom for a moment and reached up to his face and pulled him in for a kiss. All time stopped, and the camera faded away.

That was, until she said, "Wait, I didn't get that. One more time?"

I threw my head back and groaned.

"One more time!" Easton agreed.

I laughed, and he devoured my face, making ridiculous animalistic sounds, and the camera snapped over and over again.

"OK, Mom, we've got to go before it starts raining!"

We said goodbye to my mom and promised to see her that night for dinner. Only I knew it was something more than that. I'd overheard her and Easton talking about it. She was planning some sort of reception for us. I had to make the internal decision not to fight it. I would have to act surprised too. That was something I wasn't good at, but I hoped I could pull it off.

I slipped on some flats—I wasn't going to walk through the field in heels—and my mom handed me a jacket. I scowled when I realized it would clash, but I took it anyway. Easton and I both sighed in relief as the car doors shut and we were finally to ourselves.

"You look absolutely stunning, and if we didn't have to beat this storm, I would have taken you upstairs to ravish you," Easton said.

I giggled. "*After* my mom left."

"Yes! *After!*" Easton's eyes widened with his smile.

Though it was now the seventh of May, the wet weather of April had lingered. Perhaps it was the last storm of the season. The sky that was once on the cusp of turning warm earlier in the week was now grey and chilly. The condensation lingered in the air like a low-hanging cloud. We drove over the New River Bridge, my gaze glued to the very spot we met. I turned my focus to Easton.

"Why were you going to jump that day?" I was confident now that after everything I knew, he would finally tell me the truth.

Easton grabbed my hand and brought it to his lips for a warm kiss.

"When you've lived as much as I have, it's easy to become picky. I no longer live past my twenties. I choose not to. Being old is hard work. Your mind starts to slip, which can be difficult for someone, such as me. I have a lot of memories; it can be messy when reality turns into a spectrum. Plus, your vision starts to go, your body begins to ache. Things that used to be fun, just aren't anymore. That's why I prefer to live my lives basking in the glow of youth. Then, I choose to start over. Go back."

"That's so sad!"

"Yeah, it is. But I can't continue into my thirties. That's when families start. It's just not my place."

"You've never had a family?"

"No. Not until now." Easton looked over at me with a warm smile.

We pulled into the same spot we did the time we were almost eaten by bears. Our campsite was now unrecognizable with new growth. We got out of the car, and I slid my arms into my jacket. A part of me wondered why I even bothered with a dress in the first place. I was chilled from head to toe.

Hand in hand, Easton and I waded through the tall wet

grass. And all the while, his winged dragonfly remained by his side.

"Oh my God! I think that's the same one as last time!"

"It is," Easton said.

I could tell there was more to the story, judging by his calm demeanor.

"And? Are you going to tell me? Or leave me guessing?"

Easton laughed. "It's a loved one. From time to time, they visit after they've passed on. Sometimes it's a dragonfly; sometimes it's a sunset painted just for me; And sometimes it's as simple as a draft in stale air."

"You're telling me your ex-girlfriend is coming to our wedding?"

Easton laughed louder. "No! It's not my ex-girlfriend."

I giggled, stepping over a fallen tree. My dress soaking up the dew and becoming wet against my legs.

"Have you ever gotten chills? Goosebumps out of nowhere, and you knew it was something. Or someone?"

I nodded. "I've felt it. It's like that thing you can't explain?"

"Yeah! That's it! That's the bond you've shared with someone that still exists when they don't."

I thought about all the times I felt the presence of someone that wasn't there. The times I was so captivated by a bird in flight or the beauty of a sunset. I wondered how I would show myself to Easton in the years to come.

We approached the clearing where Easton confessed his life's secret to me. The dead tree was lit with twinkling lights that glowed through the thick grey fog like fireflies. White roses covered a stand-alone trellis, and music played softly into the air. Not a soul in sight. My heart skipped as I cupped my hands around my open mouth.

"What's this?" Tears pricked the corners of my eyes.

"Beck, you have a lot of people that love you."

Easton tucked my hair behind my shoulder and leaned down for a kiss full of magic and wonder. I'd never felt so loved in my entire life. The chills from my wet dress melted away with the beauty of our spot. It was majestic and spellbinding, like a fairy tale made for me. The dead tree was brought back to life with the love of my family and friends.

I picked up a rose from the arched trellis and breathed it in as I looked out to the Truly River. It was invisible due to the cloud cover, but that didn't make it any less beautiful. I was nearly convinced I could step off the cliffside, and the low hanging clouds would carry my weight. I wondered what it would be like to nestle into the plushness of a cool cloud and fall asleep. I turned to Easton as he was setting up a tripod and a video camera.

"What are you doing?" I asked as I ran the thornless rose through my hands.

"It was at the request of your parents. The only way they were willing to accept our privacy for today was to capture it on film. They wanted to have a movie made of it," Easton said.

"So, I have to wait to consumate our marriage. Is that what you're telling me?"

Easton laughed. "Well, I'm sure there's an *off* button around here somewhere!" he said with a blush.

He pushed record and joined me under the trellis. His

hair, weighted down by the moisture, fell to the sides of his eyes, making them look more vivid in contrast. I wrapped my arms around his waist and rested my head on his chest. I closed my eyes and listened to the soft playing music. "Surrender" by Natalie Taylor. The words—"My love will find you"—floated around us. Easton began to rock us into a slow dance. Our feet never left the ground.

"Easton, you found me. And for that, I'm so thankful. But for the life of me, I can't figure out, why now?" I dug my chin into his chest and gazed up into his eyes.

"I've been looking for you, for a very, very long time." His fingers twisted in the back of my hair as he spoke. "I can't tell you why now. All I know is, we were meant for each other. And I wouldn't have it any other way, no matter how short our time."

"Same."

"Visit me? If you can," Easton asked.

"You mean like a dragonfly?"

"In your own way. Whatever you choose. I'll know it's you," he said.

"I promise." My voice came out horse, the tone splintered.

Easton squeezed me tightly, and his chin began to quiver. I buried my face against him wanting to crawl inside and live there forever. Maybe I would. Live inside his heart. Perhaps that would be the only place I existed after this.

With a heavy heart, Easton pulled me away and lowered onto one knee. I took a step back as he opened a small box between us. A single oval diamond sparkled against the blue felt of the box. The light danced inside the diamond as Easton's hands trembled.

"I can't tell you I know what the future holds. I don't know. But if I know one thing, it's that I will never stop loving you. If you let me, I'll carry a piece of you with me, wherever I go."

I dabbed the tears in the corners of my eyes with shaky hands.

"Yes! Absolutely! Take as much of me as you can fit. Take it all! I want to stay with you forever," I said to Easton, and anyone else who was listening that may grant such a wish.

Easton took the ring and threw the box over his shoulder. We both chuckled as he slid the diamond ring onto my ring finger. It was a perfect fit.

"I love you," I said.

"I love you, Beck." Easton wiped away a tear with the sleeve of his jacket. Then, with one quick sweep, he lifted me into his arms and swung me around, dipping me backward towards the camera.

"She's mine! All mine! Mrs. Green!" Easton shouted to the video recorder. I giggled like a schoolgirl. Of course, we weren't legally married, nor was I legally changing my name. It was so much more than that. Something documentation could never touch.

Easton spun me around until I couldn't take anymore, and I begged him to stop. By the time my feet touched the ground, my head had continued to swim. My vision was just becoming sharp when I saw Easton shaking a bottle of champagne.

"No!"

He popped the cork, and champagne exploded into the air and rained down upon us. I screamed and took off, running behind the old dead tree. Easton chased me, spraying every last drop he could. The taste of almond champagne dripped from my hair and down onto my lips.

We ran around the tree like kids in love. The bottom half of my dress tinged with the color of earth and bark embedded into the lace. By the time Easton caught me, I was begging to be captured. I made myself clumsy just enough to fall to the ground in a bed of tall grass. Of course, he would never let me fall alone. I laid my curled hair onto the ground and searched his eyes as he realized that the fall was merely a ploy. I bit my bottom lip and his head whipped around to examine the camera's position.

"Are we out of sight?" I asked.

"Uh-huh." Easton said, breathing harder now than when he was chasing me.

Excitement sparked in his eyes as his lips crashed into mine, our love manifesting in its own celebration. One that would leave me too much of a mess for my surprise reception. Perhaps, I should have thought of that before I enticed Easton to make love to me on the forest floor underneath a tower of roses and fairy lights. Although, I assured myself it wouldn't have changed anything.

I lay, basking in the afterglow, on his outreached arm. My legs were itchy from the grass, and I watched the misty grey clouds dance through the sky. We talked about life until the first drops of rain crashed down on us.

"We should go," Easton said, looking at me.

I sighed and turned to look back at him. Our noses were nearly touching and grass was peaking up all around us.

"I guess it's time," I said. I didn't want to leave.

Easton helped me up, and I made it to my feet. My balance off for a minute or two. He collected the small speaker and camera and turned them off.

"They'll never know," Easton said as he placed the camera in his jacket pocket.

"Do we leave all this here?" I asked. The raindrops coming more frequently.

"Yeah! They'll come to clean it up tomorrow. Come on, let's go. We still have to hike out!"

By the time we reached the car, it didn't matter that my dress was soaked in champagne and I had grass stains riding up the back. We were drenching wet. Same as the night I met Easton.

"Déjà vu!" I said after slamming the car door closed.

Easton laughed, "Who would have thought on that stormy evening that we would be married by May."

"Me," I said.

"Oh! Come on! You didn't know what you thought of me!" Easton laughed.

I echoed his laughter.

"That's not true! I thought you were deranged! And most likely homeless . . ."

I giggled, knowing that Easton was appalled by my honesty. I bet he never saw that one coming. I pulled down the sun visor and checked myself in the mirror. I looked like a drowned rat.

"Good Lord! I can't go to my parent's house like this!"

Easton tried to be supportive. He tried to hold in his amusement, but my white dress was green with lover's passion. He burst into laughter.

"We'll make a pit stop. Two, actually. I should change too! I'll just text your mom that we're going to run a little late."

"OK, good call. Hopefully we're not too late though. I would feel bad."

I turned the heat on and kicked off my wet shoes. Huddling into a ball for warmth near the vent.

"Think you will move some of your stuff in?" I asked.

"I've been sneaking some things over slowly. It feels weird to be at my place now. It doesn't even feel like home!"

"And my place does?"

"*You* feel like home. And your place is covered in your things. It's comforting," Easton said.

Thunder cracked, and the sky lit up in a brilliant blue seconds later. I watched the electricity dance outside my window like a show made only for my eyes. Nature had never been so beautiful to me as it was in the last couple of weeks. The colors of the earth had never been so brilliant.

We continued our drive talking about what he would move over and what he would do with his place now that it would be vacant. I tried to coax him into telling me what my mom had planned for the surprise reception, but he was a stubborn one and wouldn't budge.

"Next week, if you're up for it, let's take a trip."

"Where to?" I asked.

"The beach. I want to get you on that horse, and we can

gallop through the water! Do you still want to do that?" he asked.

"I forgot about that!" I looked into the sky, waiting for the next light show. "Hey, do you still have that menu?" I asked.

"Yeah, it should be in the glove box." Easton motioned to the compartment before me.

I opened it, and the to-go menu of Hunters fell to the floor. I marveled at the markings: only my bucket list items, none of his. Now I knew why. He'd done everything that he ever wanted to do, and then some. Getting married was probably one of the first "firsts" he'd had in a long time.

"Oh! The northern lights sound pretty good too!" I said, even more interested than the day I mentioned it. I picked up a pen and scratched off "get married."

"Which one did you mark off?" Easton asked.

"Get married. Oh! And dance at my wedding. You wrote that?" I asked as I drove a line through it.

"I barely remember saying it," I confessed.

I coughed, struggling to clear my throat. It wasn't until I pulled my hand away that I saw the bright red blood and tasted the copper in my mouth. I froze, not quite understanding why my hand was painted red. Easton's eyes flickered over to me and I hid my hand in my lap, ashamed. Streaks of blood now on my white dress. I felt Easton's concern, but I didn't look. Not until I heard it.

A horn sounded, long and loud, until the screeching of the tires became deafening. I lifted my head just in time to see the semi plow into the front passenger's side of our car. The headlights blinding the rain-soaked windows. The impact jarring as it sent us through the guard rails of the New River Bridge.

And just for a moment, time seemed to still. The free fall in slow motion as Easton's car plummeted to the river below. All I remained concerned with was hiding my blood-stained hand. The realization that my life was ending there and now had not yet registered.

The force of the crash knocked me half unconscious. I was barely aware that Easton was trying everything he could to free me from my seat belt. But the doors were totaled and fused shut. My seatbelt was jammed. And the same blood on my hand that I'd been desperately trying to hide, now spilled from my head as well.

Ice cold water was rushing in as Easton panicked around me. My consciousness slipping. My fate had found me. It wasn't until the water trickled up to my nose, did I regain full awareness—my adrenaline making one last lap. I struggled to free myself, but couldn't. I tried to hold my breath as the water swallowed me whole.

And there he was. Easton, by my side. His seatbelt free, and his window kicked through. He stayed. I didn't want that for him. And watching his life end was far worse than leaving my body behind. But in these last fleeting moments, I admittedly was comforted by his presence.

As I stared into Easton's eyes through the cold river water on my last breath, hundreds of images flooded my mind. My brother, giving me his last hug. My parents, handing me flowers after my dance recital when I was seven. Easton's shoes hanging off the guardrail of the New River Bridge. The smell of puppy breath and the taste of almond champagne kisses. All as real as if they were happening in the present moment.

I saw the reception at my parent's house. I watched as my mom fell to the floor when the cops told her the news. My reception turning into an impromptu funeral. I wondered if the camera would ever be found, and what picture they would choose to blow up at my service. I hoped it would be the one of Easton kissing me while I laughed wholeheartedly. I bet that was a good one.

My body protested the lack of oxygen. I gasped for air, and ice water rushed into my lungs. I watched the little bubbles escape Easton's nose until I could no longer feel the cold in my extremities. Easton faded away into a sea of darkness, and my mind was finally at rest. I used to think dying was the worst thing that could happen to a person. As it turns out, it's not . . .

Passing away is actually quite natural. I knew how to do it without ever practicing.

Two months ago, I thought the angels were crying for me. One month ago, I knew they were crying for Easton. What I would later come to realize was, they were never crying at all. They were merely washing away the mistakes —the broken and defective. Cleaning the slate for something new. Something better. I would come to understand that this wasn't the end of my life . . . but only the very beginning.

Thank you for reading. Please consider leaving a review.

Your feedback is the best way to help me succeed as a new author and I appreciate you taking the time to leave a quick review or star rating.

Xoxo,
Laura C. Reden

ABOUT THE AUTHOR

Laura C. Reden is an emerging romance author who likes to add paranormal and fantasy twists while tugging at the heart strings.

Overcoming the struggles of dyslexia, Laura found that creative passion and hard work triumphs over her disadvantage.

Laura is a Southern Californian native, wife, and mother of two daughters. Her pastimes include video production, pottery, and horseback riding. While she received an education in social and behavioral science, she currently works as the chief financial officer for her family-owned law firm in San Diego.

If you are interested in staying updated on new releases, subscribe to my monthly email list. It's short and sweet with opportunities to help name characters, get advanced review copies, and even have your pet featured in upcoming scenes.

https://www.subscribepage.com/redenbooks

Xoxo,

Laura

ALSO BY

YOU'VE HEARD THE TERM «OLD SOUL» BEFORE,
BUT WHAT IF SOME SOULS NEVER REALLY DIE?

THE TETHERED SOUL SERIES

FOLLOW THE TRAGIC TALE OF A DYING GIRL,
AND BOY WITH AN IMMORTAL SOUL.

LAURA C. REDEN

DREAMS ARE FICKLE, EMOTIONS ARE BOLD.

THE
PHANTOM SERIES

CAUGHT BETWEEN WORLDS,
KINSLEY WILDE CAN SEE THE DEAD,
MANIFEST HER DREAMS, AND CONJURE HER FEARS.

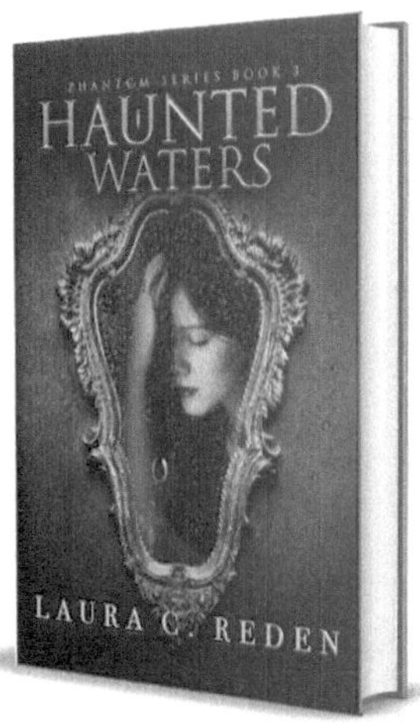

BOOK CLUB NOTES

BOOK CLUB NOTES

www.ingramcontent.com/pod-product-compliance
Lightning Source LLC
Chambersburg PA
CBHW061605190726
48288CB00007B/2191